The Sun Rises Over Seven Sisters

By

M.L. Bullock

Dedication

To the ghosts of the South, we remember you.

MIDNIGHT has come, and the great Christ Church Bell
And may a lesser bell sound through the room;
And it is All Souls' Night,
And two long glasses brimmed with muscatel
Bubble upon the table.

A ghost may come;
For it is a ghost's right,
His element is so fine
Being sharpened by his death,
To drink from the wine-breath
While our gross palates drink from the whole wine.

—William Butler Yeats
"All Souls' Night"
Autumn 1920

Prologue—Isla

This morning's chilly air had long since evaporated, replaced by the pungent fragrance of the nearby docks. No cool breeze blew off the water. Not one strong enough to wind through the stale rooms of the Holy Angels Sanitarium. I supposed building the hospital near the Mobile Bay was meant to soothe the facility's patients, but it did not bring that kind of relief for me. The eternal slapping of the water on the shore and the constant churning of the steamboats passing by made me think of my Sweet Captain.

Oh, mon amour! How I miss you! Rescue me, my darling! Take me in your arms once again!

Never had I met a man so beautiful and amiable. So far above all others. Until he failed, and then all of heaven wept at his fall. I was sure some lovely angel with long limbs and golden skin was loving him even now, and the thought of it filled me with anger all over again. Yes, in the end he had been like all the others. Unfaithful to the bone was he, and the fact I missed him so only reflected on my poor character.

Yet, I did miss him. Especially during the quiet moments of the day. Wouldn't any wife miss her husband? Even an unfaithful one?

I could not think of him now. Not with so much to plan.

I would never give up my claim on Seven Sisters. It was mine now, that and the Beaumont fortune. They would both be mine! I clamped my lips together in determination.

One of the dull girls who shared a room with me—Angela, I believe her name was—muffled a cry at the sight of my grimaced face, but she did not speak to me. She knew better. Yes, she had learned that quickly, in spite of her madness. We shuffled down the hall to eat our morning meal, looking like a string of prostitutes, our hair unbound, gowns hanging loosely. The guards made the women here surrender their ribbons and corset ties for fear we might hang ourselves. Who ever heard of doing yourself in with a corset ribbon? I could not imagine ever doing such a thing, but then I was not the kind of woman to take her own life. I might be compelled to take the lives of others. Whenever necessary.

I had a clever mind, but I would remove anyone who stood in my way. It was as simple as that. I tried to explain all this to the physician. When I saw I shocked him, I used my prettiest pout and even twisted my hair playfully, but he was not moved. After a few hours of constant interviewing, I told him what I thought about him and demanded that he release me.

"My dear lady, I did not put you here. You are a ward of the city now and due to stand trial. Only the judge can issue a release, so I suggest you make yourself comfortable. Take time to reflect upon your deeds, and perhaps the judge will have mercy on you." I knocked over his ink well and slapped his papers around before he yelled for the guard. Upon later reflection I realized that I had been foolish to act so rashly, but I felt sure I could persuade Dr. Hannah to petition the court on my behalf. I was still pretty. I had charms and skills that many women did not. From that day forward I did not stir up the staff or the other patients. Not openly, at any rate.

After stuffing a piece of dry biscuit into my mouth and swallowing a few gulps of water, I walked into the open yard looking for a quiet place where I could sit alone. How I longed to have a meal that required a knife and fork. Never would I enjoy that here. I could not abide the company of such madwomen! Even now they were behaving like idiot children. One of them, a tall, thin wisp of a woman, slapped her own face constantly. She had near permanent red marks on her cheeks. Most days, a guard would eventually tire of her self-destruction and tie her hands together. Then she would sit and moan and whine until bedtime. If anyone cared to listen, they would hear her repeat the same phrase, "My boy, Dimitri. My boy, Dimitri." She had a heavy Russian accent; I had heard it before during my travels with my captain!

Oh, David! How I miss you! What will become of me now, my love?

Another patient always pulled at the hem of her sleeve or dress. She pulled away inches of fabric every day and seemed absolutely riveted by the destruction. In the short time I had been at Holy Angels Sanitarium, she had been issued two garments, both essentially sacks made to look like dresses. I did not think she minded much because she quickly unwound them and then sat naked, crying that she had nothing to do. Mrs. Ambrosia, she was called, and she appeared as if she would come sit by me this morning with her missing sleeve and hem to the knees. I hissed at her under my breath to discourage her without making an open fuss.

She took the hint and wandered off in the other direction, tugging at the string on her sleeve.

Now, where was I? I said to no one in particular. I stared at the nearby waters of the Mobile Bay from behind the cast-iron bars. I made plans for after this unnecessary excursion. A girl had to have plans, didn't she? I was always a girl with a plan. I would demand, pleasantly, to see the physician tomorrow. I would apologize most humbly and explain to him the great distress I had been in since the death of my husband. He would understand. Men always understood pretty faces.

I frowned into the sun and closed my eyes. Where had Docie been? She had visited me only once, and even then she acted as if she did not want to linger too long. I suspected my former maid had vanished—probably with my remaining fortune. That would be a mistake for her. I treasured loyalty above all things.

The sound of mewing pulled me back to my present circumstance. I had seen the kitten before, but it had not amused me to help it in any way. Fortunately for the lost feline, my situation had changed. I knelt on the ground near the fence and pulled a few biscuit crumbs from my pocket. I knew the guard was watching me, for he always watched me, but thus far he had been careful to keep his distance and had not spoken to me directly. He was a portly man with a bushy brown mustache and thinning hair. Just from observing him I could tell he was secretive and quiet. Those men were the most dangerous kind because they were hard to predict and sometimes hard to please, but he did not frighten me. I pushed the biscuit pieces through the metal bars and spoke sweetly to the animal. Hunger drove it to trust me at least long enough to accept my offerings. It was a sad-looking tabby cat, underweight with missing patches of hair. I did not imagine it would live very long, but anything was possible.

After it got a taste of the biscuit, it naturally wanted more. I pretended I had not noticed the guard step closer to observe me. I held another piece of biscuit out for the kitten to see but put it in my lap. I let the loose gown fall from my shoulder, exposing my skin. Since I was pretending that I did not see the guard, I did not bother to tug it back into place. I kept my eyes on the kitten, who was not cooperating too well. If it wanted something to eat, it would have to take a chance. "It's okay, Mr. Buttons," I purred loudly enough for the guard to hear, "you can trust me."

"What do you plan on doing with that animal? You cannot bring it in here, miss."

Artfully placing my dainty hand over my eyes, I peered into his face with my most innocent expression. "Oh no, sir. I have no intention of keeping him. I only meant to help him along a bit. Look how small and helpless he is."

"Keep that cat out of the yard, miss."

"Oh, have I broken a rule, sir?" I turned my upper body, arching my back slightly, and my hand flew to my mouth as if I were surprised. "Forgive me. May I toss the last of my crumbs to the poor thing?"

He shuffled his feet and hesitated but finally said, "Yes, you may."

"Thank you, sir. Here, Mr. Buttons."

I tossed the crumbs through the gate and stood clumsily, pretending I might trip and fall on my loose gown. His hands quickly went out to steady me, and I did not push them away. "Again, I thank you," I whispered as a small smile spread across my face. I did not meet his eyes but looked at his hand as he removed it nervously. This was too easy. I did not know yet what my plan was, but I felt sure that if I needed to, I would be able to call upon the very helpful guard. Who knows? Maybe Dr. Hannah would not see reason and release me. In that case, I would need help from someone else. I left the guard to watch me walk away, looking back once over my shoulder to give him a demure smile. I picked up the skirts of my untied dress just as I would if I were climbing the steps at Seven Sisters.

He did not follow me. The lady warden, a stern woman named Miss Calypso, came toward me, her shiny black kid boots clicking on the grimy floor. "Miss Beaumont, you have a visitor."

"I have a visitor?" I could not hide my surprise.

"Your mother has come to see you. Straighten your dress and make yourself presentable. As presentable as you get, anyway. The physician has given you permission to sit in the private yard to speak with her. This way, miss."

I thanked Miss Calypso politely and followed her. How clever of Docie to claim to be my mother! Surely she could manage that disguise! She had seen me on the stage for years pretending to be Ophelia, Lady Macbeth and a dozen other characters. I smiled more, thinking of what her choice of disguise might be. Would she have colored her hair? Surely she would not have borrowed a gown, for she did not fit into my clothes at all.

I stepped through the physician's office, and he greeted me briefly. I could tell by his suspicious look and tone that he had not yet forgiven me for my outburst the week before. The lady warden opened the door that led to the doctor's private garden. It was a meager garden at best, but it did have a pleasant shade tree, a young magnolia, two benches and a few scant patches of Bourbon roses. My eyes were on none of these but on the woman who sat on the farthest bench. Her cold blue eyes clamped on my face. This was certainly not Docie, and I could not place her although she was familiar to me in some way. Perhaps she was a fan of my work? I smiled pleasantly, but it was not returned. She studied me as she rose from her peaceful spot in the shade of the tree. She came closer, and the unsettled feeling climbed up my spine.

This woman was my mother.

There we stood appraising one another, not in an overtly threatening manner, just curious. One would have imagined that I would have questions, and perhaps someone other than myself would have been overwhelmed with love or sadness. I experienced none of those things. It did not occur to me to wonder what she might be thinking. Did that matter? I knew one thing—she had been a fool for sending me away. I was beautiful, intelligent and clever at solving puzzles.

Olivia Beaumont had a chiseled, lovely face for an older woman. She must have been at least forty, but she was far lovelier than her sister Christine had been. Olivia had dark blond hair that appeared to have been tinted recently, perhaps to hide silver strands? I smiled at that. She wore it in an upswept, feminine fashion like the women in London. Her hairstyle held plenty of decorative pins, and she wore carefully placed curls at her neck and ears.

I wondered what she would do if I told her about her brother, how he died beaten in the head with a garden curiosity by his brother-in-law's young black lover. *Worm food now, I suppose.* Would she collapse into a pile and whimper as her fragile sister had? I knew she would not. She was not a frail thing but someone with a will and soul of steel, despite her lacy appearance.

Her lips were carefully painted a dark color, but it did not make her look a whore. It made her light blue eyes lovelier and more expressive. At her ears were modest pearls, and her gown was also in the London style with a smaller bustle than the hoopskirts we Southern women were forced to endure. So was she more than a fashion plate? She appeared wealthy and lovely, like a great woman should. I wondered how she came to be here. Who had summoned her to the Holy Angels Sanitarium?

There we were, mother and daughter, standing in a sparse garden and silently staring at one another. I suddenly felt foolish for looking so out of sorts. When had I last bathed? When had I washed my hair? She seemed not to notice those things but instead focused on my face.

"Ah, thank you for waiting, ladies. I did not mean to be so long." It was Dr. Hannah, the tall, fleshy physician with the white hair and the monocle. His pale skin had a touch of pinkness, like a baby's or an albino rat's. I suppressed a giggle at the thought of Dr. Hannah as a rat. Olivia stared at me, her blue eyes like two glass marbles that could see right through me. I quieted and sat with my hands folded in my lap, just as I had learned from Christine and Calpurnia.

"Thank you for coming, Mrs. Torrence. How disappointing that I will not meet your husband. Typhoid, is it? Very nasty illness, that. If I were you, I would keep far away from home until he is completely clear of the disease."

Abruptly she stood and interrupted his speech. "Would you mind if I had a few minutes alone with Isla? As you can imagine, we have many private things to speak of."

With a serious pursing of his lips he answered her, "Certainly, Mrs. Torrence. I will be in the office if you need me. I would like to speak to the two of you together, but there is no need to hurry. Take your time."

"In fact—Dr. Hannah, is it? We will not be speaking with you at all, today or any other day. This is for you." She handed the man a scroll of papers. He could not hide his surprise as he scanned the documents.

"Everything looks to be in order, but I am afraid I haven't yet completed my examination of Miss Beaumont. This is most irregular." His objections availed him nothing, and he knew it after a few more stern looks. "Will you be leaving right away?" Olivia stared at him as if he were the mental patient. He sputtered and stammered, "Yes, of course you will be. Very well, I will ask the warden to collect your daughter's things. Good day to you then, Mrs. Torrence." She did not smile or thank him, just watched him disappear back into the white painted building.

I marveled at the whole thing. I had planned to seduce my way to freedom, but Olivia wielded a power I had never seen before, all without saying please or smiling even once. I wanted to learn how to use this power. I wondered if she would share it with me.

"Now you and I need to talk."

"Yes, Mother," I said sweetly.

"Drop the act. Do not call me Mother. I am not your mother. I am your aunt. You may call me Mrs. Torrence."

Now I felt like Dr. Hannah, completely unprepared to withstand Olivia's stare and authoritative manner.

"Your mother was a common street woman from New Orleans, a woman who convinced my brother that he was your father. He was foolish to believe so, but he did."

"What do you mean you are not my mother? I have always been told that you were. How can this be wrong?" I frowned in suspicion.

"I am not. I would think I would know whether or not you were mine." No smile, no expression of sadness or regret. No expression at all. To her, this was a boring conversation forced upon her by the judge who had summoned her to speak on my behalf. Or so I assumed.

"Then why the charade with the judge and the physician?"

"Why not? It is what they believe, so who am I to tell them different? I refuse to share family gossip with them or shame my family further."

I stepped toward her, uncaring that my gown had fallen off my shoulder again. "What about the shame it brought on you? Having a cast-off child, having me believe you did not want me as your daughter."

"It is my brother who should feel the shame. On the other hand, he is dead, so I doubt he feels much of anything." I gasped at her total lack of concern for my feelings on this matter. "Are you going to cry now? If so, do me the courtesy of waiting until we are in the carriage. I cannot abide public outbursts."

Sniffing away the wash of emotions, I answered her confidently, "I will not make a fuss."

She appraised me again. "I *should* leave you here. I am sure you could finagle your way out if you chose to. Probably already have a plan, don't you?"

I should never have admitted it, but I nodded slowly.

"Yes, you are your father's child. Scheming and planning. Let us go now."

"Where are we going, Mrs. Torrence?"

"To Seven Sisters, of course. I want to see what's become of my sister's fortune. You sure have made a mess of things, haven't you?" She walked toward the door, but I had to correct her. I had done everything—everything imaginable—to keep the family fortune. I would not let this slight pass.

"No! Your sister did that by having two children out of wedlock. Cottonwood knew all about it. However..." I smiled proudly here. I was anxious for her to respect me. *No need to wait. Let us establish the facts now*, I told myself. "He has left everything to his rightful heir, my own daughter, Karah Cottonwood."

Olivia's hard stare elicited another sentence from my lips. It was probably not wise to say aloud, but the words came anyway. "That leaves nothing to the Beaumonts, I'm afraid."

"Is that what you truly believe?" she asked, her face a pretty, unemotional mask. It wasn't really a question; it was more of a challenge. "My carriage is outside." She walked into the office, down the hall and out the door without looking back once. Good thing for her she didn't. I stuck out my tongue at her at least a half dozen times during the trek to the entrance. To my surprise the raggedy-looking tabby cat waited for us as if he too wanted to escape. He rubbed against my leg as if I were his only friend. Perhaps I was. More was the pity for him.

Olivia eyed me as I petted him once. "Your pet?"

"Hardly," I answered as I climbed into the carriage behind her. I was ready to go home and take a bath, eat real food and find a new dress. I watched Mrs. Torrence as she instructed the driver which way to go. Frigidity masked as decorum. Did she think I would be intimidated by her folded hands, her elegant kid gloves? I looked down into my own hands. Broken nails with dirty beds and torn skin. I stared at them intently. I did not hide them. Maybe these weren't the hands of a lady, but they were the hands of a fighter, someone accustomed to fighting for everything.

I could feel her cold eyes on me, but still I smiled at my hands.

No, these hands would not let me down.

We would fight, and we would win.

Chapter One—Carrie Jo

The tap on the front door woke me from my nap. That was aggravating, as I could just feel myself slip away into a pleasant dream. With my recent influx of nightmares and sleep paralysis, dreaming about something nice would be a godsend. Thankfully I was no longer invading my husband's dreams. I shuddered to think about what he would be dreaming now that I was as big as a house. Although our love and commitment to one another remained strong, Ashland and I argued a lot lately. The worst part was, our disagreements, as he called them, were mostly over insignificant things like who misplaced the hammer or how the puppy got out. As I reminded him frequently, the new dog had been his idea and I never used the hammer. Well, hardly ever. I did hang a baby calendar in my office. And I found some cute wooden monograms to hang in my room.

Ashland's dog, a cute white Maltese, demanded constant affection and attention, and quite frankly he was a lousy watchdog. In fact, he was in full-blown nap mode at the foot of the couch when the visitor came to my door. He hadn't even budged at the knock. *Yeah, right. Big-time watchdog. Thanks, fella.*

Ashland and I would have to talk about that later. Well, maybe not. I think we had fulfilled our mandatory couple's argument quota for the year. Especially after last night. That had been the fight of the century, and I couldn't understand it. Why was Ash being so unreasonable? Apparently the subject of baby names was a hill that both of us were willing to die on. He hated the idea of naming our child anything "old-fashioned." I hated the idea of giving our son or daughter this year's trendiest name. Well, it couldn't be as bad as Carrie Jo. What had my mother been thinking?

"Just a second," I called to the unscheduled visitor who tapped again at the door. I tossed the soft throw blanket to the side and slid carefully off the couch. Navigating life with a big old baby belly had proved a challenge, but I liked being pregnant. Whenever he or she arrived (I still held out hope for a girl) I would miss this experience. The closeness with my child, the feeling of life growing inside me. It was like my love with Ashland had created a bit of magic, and now that magic would become an amazing person. "Whatever, Carrie Jo," I muttered to myself. I had become too sentimental lately. Too many sappy movies.

Peeking through the glass door, I could see the mail lady waiting patiently for me. I arranged my sloppy t-shirt and flyaway hair before opening the door with a smile.

"Good morning! These are for you, Mrs. Stuart." I accepted the bundle of letters and the package she handed me. I dropped a few items, but she graciously picked them up for me. No way was I going to bend down, not without some help getting up.

"Thanks. Anything good in there?"

"More baby catalogs. Almost time, isn't it?" Sharone Pugh and I had become quite familiar with one another the past few months. Too many late nights spent shopping online for baby clothes, furniture and whatever else struck my fancy. Sharone showed up day after day with something new. I gave up apologizing after a while. She didn't complain. Not too much, anyway. I joked with her that I would have the best-dressed infant in downtown Mobile, but at this point the only colors in the child's wardrobe were yellow and white. (Lenore had declared we would have a boy, but I wasn't so sure.)

"Can you believe my doctor says three more weeks? I don't think it's humanly possible to get any bigger."

"I was as big as a hippo when I delivered my first child. Gained seventy pounds too. You look wonderful. I'd better go. I have a ton of mail to deliver, and I can't leave my truck on the street. Have a nice day." She walked away as I said goodbye.

Closing the door behind me, I set the package on the foyer table and flipped through the stack of envelopes. The third letter in, I froze. It was from my mother. I stared at her name written in the familiar handwriting.

Deidre Jardine

Dumping the rest of the mail on the table with the package, I took the letter with trembling hands, grabbed the blanket and plopped back on the couch. As if he or she knew my heart was pounding, the baby turned in my tummy and pressed on my bladder. "Hey, cut that out, kiddo." After a few seconds the baby got comfortable again, and I leaned back on the pillow hoping to get some relief from the dull ache in my side. The clock struck half past the hour. It was 9:30 on Saturday morning, just a few hours before the baby shower. Plenty of time to take a nap. Ashland would not be back from his latest deposition for a while, and lately he had been in no mood to just hang out. I tried to be understanding, but I'd had my own crankiness to deal with. I blamed it on the pregnancy, but I knew it was stress. For the past six months Ash had been battered with lawsuits about the most mundane things, from claims on the estate to an unhappy tenant who claimed he was a slumlord.

And now this letter.

It was just one more thing. What could she possibly have to say to me? We had not spoken, emailed or messaged one another in over two years. Sure, I had stared at her contact info in my phone a few times, but I never actually called. Then again, she never called me either. Feeling tired and tearful, I put the letter on the coffee table and lay down again. The house was quiet, and there were no shadows. Maybe it would be safe to sleep. Safe to dream. I needed the rest. I could read the letter later. I touched it once again and then wrapped the blanket around my shoulders and snuggled into the plush couch. I had so many reasons to be happy. So why was I so unhappy? I told my mind to be quiet, and after a few more minutes of unhappy rumination I fell asleep.

***

Olivia Torrence had spoken barely a word on our journey to Seven Sisters. Obviously she had been here before. She did not crane her neck out the carriage window or gawk up at the white-painted edifice that shone brightly in the late morning sunlight. She was not overawed by the sheer size of the plantation or the obvious wealth that commanded it. I reminded myself that Olivia Beaumont Torrence was probably the wealthiest woman I had ever met. If I could have her as my ally, then who could stop me? But for that to happen, I would have to show her I was worthy of her partnership. No flattering words or innocent smiles for her. She would appreciate intelligence. I had to show her I was worthy of her trust.

The carriage shifted, and I slid across the seat. I noticed that she had barely moved a muscle. How was that possible? Was she made of stone or marble? She did remind me of the statues in the Moonlight Garden. Elegant, pale and forever frozen in one position. Despite the uncomfortable nature of our silence, I refused to be the first to speak. Instead, I peeked out the window at the house, uncaring that she thought me a fool. Once the carriage arrived, Stokes came to the door and pushed the latch, freeing me from my latest prison. It was good to be home! This was my home! I had broken every commandment in the Holy Bible to have this place, and I would not be denied. Not now and not ever. Hooney lingered in the doorway, but she did not offer a glass of lemonade or a bite to eat.

I frowned at her, and she made the sign of the cross. I laughed and strolled into the house like I owned it. Over my shoulder I said to Mrs. Torrence, "Forgive me, Aunt. I need to bathe and change. It has been far too long since I had a proper scrub."

She slid off her gloves and ignored me, which aggravated me to no end. She strolled into the ladies' parlor with Stokes on her heels. I heard her speaking to him in low tones, and I stomped up the stairs happy to be out of her company. "Hooney! I need a bath. Send someone up here with some hot water." She also did not answer, but I noticed she shuffled her old feet to fulfill my request. What did I care if she carried the water up herself? I doubted she would, though. Soon I heard wood being tossed in the upstairs stove and the sloshing of water. When the water was heated, I would soak my bones and wash away my cares.

I had claimed Christine's old room. Seemed appropriate—this was where the lady of the house slept, wasn't it? To my utter shock and amazement, all my things had been packed in trunks, stuffed away like yesterday's rubbish. "Hooney!" I yelled in my most aggravated tone. She never came. It was Hannah who came into the room, drying her hands on her yellow checked apron.

"Yes, miss?"

"I am hardly a miss, am I? Why are my things stuffed away? Look at my dresses! Everything is wrinkled. How can I wear these now? They must be pressed immediately."

"Mrs. Torrence told us to pack your things. I tried to pack them proper. I can try again. I am sorry, miss."

"What do you mean pack my things? I am not going anywhere!" I snapped at her. She looked at me, unsure about what I was saying. I shoved her out of the way and stomped out of the room. I suddenly did not care that my hair was a mess or that my dress hung off my thin, dirty shoulders.

In my bare feet I stomped into the ladies' parlor to find Olivia, but she was not there. Angrily I sailed through the Blue Room and yet again found no sign of her. Crossing the hall, I could hear her shuffling around in Jeremiah's study. She sat straight-backed in a cherrywood chair—not the master's chair, but a more petite one. She had shoved Jeremiah's monstrosity to the side as if it were something she could not abide touching. Perched on her nose were a pair of spectacles, and she was sorting through a stack of crumpled papers.

"What do you mean by having the servants pack my things? I have no plans to leave Seven Sisters."

"I am not prepared to speak with a madwoman," she said, barely breaking her gaze from the papers.

Her answer surprised me, and I sputtered for a moment. "How dare you! I am nowhere near mad. I do not know what plans you think you have for me, but I can tell you mine. I am not leaving Seven Sisters. This is my home."

She tossed her glasses on the desk and stood behind it, looking tall and rigid like an oak tree. "Speak to me like that again, and I will put you back where I found you. You are here only by my good graces. The sooner you understand that, the easier things will be."

"Easier? You have no idea what I have endured—the price I have paid."

"No more than any woman has, I am sure," she said flatly. "That is your problem. You think yourself a victim. You are weak, like most women. You are too old to play games like a spoiled schoolgirl."

Feeling the thrill of rage rise again, I smiled at her and stepped closer to the desk. I subtly searched for a weapon. My eyes fell on a letter opener with a black enamel handle.

Her perfect brows rose astutely. "See? Weak. Murder is a common solution for common minds. Imagine that I would waste my time rescuing you when I heard you described as clever! I shouldn't have bothered." Without waiting for my response, she picked up her spectacles and sat back down in the chair. She pretended to read her many papers.

"I am not leaving Seven Sisters, Aunt."

"I don't think you have much choice in the matter, do you? Dead or alive, you will do as you're told."

I stared at my aunt with a ferocious glare. How dare she judge me! Call me old, would she? She who wore a high collar and long sleeves, undoubtedly to mask her age? Should I tell her that the neck and hands were the first to go? There wasn't enough lace in the world to hide those telltale signs. She was entirely too thin, but I still had a young, firm body with plenty of soft curves. As I stood with my head held high, I caught a whiff of myself. I had the stench of the asylum on my skin. It humbled me. For a moment.

I left her without a word and went upstairs to take my bath. I needed to think and not act. How many times had my Sweet Captain reminded me of that very thing, "Think first, then act, my love." According to him, I was too spontaneous, too ready to act without first thinking through a matter. I should have taken his advice. But in the words of old Ben Franklin, it was never too late to try. I had not yet made up my mind about Olivia. Would I kill her? Rob her? Befriend her? I pondered these options as Hannah washed my hair with lemon-scented soap. The aroma was intoxicating. Then she scrubbed my feet with the bristle brush and, when I was dry, rubbed my skin with coconut oil. I felt like a debutante when her ministrations were completed.

"Dinner is almost ready, miss. You want me to help you dress? I think this pink gown is less wrinkled than the others. I promise to finish pressing the others tomorrow. I do apologize."

"No pink. Bring me the dark blue dress. The one with the blue lace on the sleeves."

A few minutes later I walked down the stairs to dine with my aunt. As I walked ever so slowly, I thought about her words. She considered me weak, but she was wrong. Oh so wrong! I had survived when she and the rest of the Beaumonts had cast me off as unworthy. And all this time I had lived. I had nothing to hang my head about. A celebrated beauty, I had traveled the world like a queen with David by my side, sometimes performing, other times watching him win his precious card games.

I took a few more steps, remembering the first time I saw David standing near this bottom step. How direct he had been! How I wanted to stare into those eyes of blue velvet forever! When we failed in our mission to lead Calpurnia into finding the Beaumont treasure, I made another plan and achieved it. My own mind had conceived those plans! None other. Still determined to win, I had a Cottonwood baby. Although she was a girl, I had delivered a promised heir. Could anyone imagine how difficult it was to seduce a man who preferred boys? I had taken great pains to capture his attentions, but I had managed it. It was easy to do with Calpurnia neatly locked away in her prison. And I had been the one who convinced Jeremiah to finish Christine. I watched him pull the rope as her body went up and up. If not for Hoyt Page, the adulterer doctor, I would have the deed to this place and plenty of freedom to find the missing jewels.

Later, when my Sweet Captain considered leaving me, I made another hard decision. Never could I forget the feeling of his warm blood seeping out of his body and into my hands. And he had never known it was me who pulled the trigger. But now he would never leave me.

I reached the bottom of the stairs and stood in the foyer of Seven Sisters. This was mine. I had made a deal with a devil named Cottonwood.

I had paid the price.

I would not be denied.

Chapter Two—Carrie Jo

I saw Lenore's face. Her dark eyes wide, she mouthed a word to me, but I could not understand her. No sound came out of her mouth. I woke with a start. The puppy yelped in surprise as my body jerked awake. "Oh, sorry, little guy. I forgot you were there." I swung my legs around and sat on the edge of the couch, my head in my hands. How was I dreaming about Isla again? I took a moment to "feel" my environment. There were no ghosts, as far as I could tell. I heard no giggles and saw no gray spirits with bloodless lips and ashen hair. But I had learned something, hadn't I? Olivia was not Isla's mother after all. Why was I seeing this now?

I did feel Lenore's presence, but only for a fleeting moment. She was here, or she had been. Warning me about something. The fat puppy whined beside me, and I stared at him. "Need to go out? Come on, chunky boy." He hopped off the couch and trotted to the door, waiting impatiently for me to get up. I glanced at the clock again. Darn! I had only 30 minutes to get ready. I told myself I'd have to think about all this later as I tried to shake off the remnants of my dream.

The puppy (I would have to give him a name sooner or later) wandered around the garden for a while, entranced by flowers, butterflies and anything that distracted him from his potty task. With some coaxing he finished his business and ran back in the house to find a snack. A snack sounded good, but I had to get going. I was sure there would be plenty to eat at my shower. Especially if Henri was involved. Man, that guy could cook! I trekked upstairs and found something mommy-ish to wear. It was kind of Detra Ann to host this shower for me, but I honestly didn't need anything. Still, it would be good to see Rachel, Detra Ann and the rest of the folks in my small circle of friends. We were like a family. We celebrated one another's birthdays and anniversaries, and we spent holidays together. In a sense, we were a band of broken people, a tribe of weirdos, each with their own supernatural power. Except perhaps Rachel, but then again I considered her research skills pretty amazing. I hoped she'd have some updates for me on that project we were working on. I was curious to see the end result. Ashland would be so surprised!

Speaking of, I hoped he remembered to show up at Detra Ann's. This was supposed to be a couple's baby shower, not just a party for me. I hoped the attorney didn't invite herself as she tended to do at times. I didn't care for her too much. She reminded me of someone, someone from my past that I couldn't trust. But I did trust my husband. He wasn't the kind of guy to be unfaithful. He hated that his father had been that sort of man. Ashland Stuart's life goals included being the complete opposite of his father. I can't say that I blamed him. His father was a terrible husband, by all accounts. In fact, two of the recent lawsuits came from two different individuals claiming to be the misbegotten sons of the late Mr. Stuart. I wondered what kind of father-in-law or grandfather he would have been. My phone dinged, and I read the text from Detra Ann.

Come on, slowpoke!

I sent a smiley emoticon back and slid my swollen feet into my sandals. I tossed my wallet, keys and makeup bag into a purse that matched my dress, then scanned myself in the mirror. I suddenly regretted my attire choice. This bright yellow dress made me look like Big Bird, but I couldn't change now. It was sleeveless with white flowers at the collar and along the hem. It was still warm out even though fall was approaching, and I wanted to wear this dress at least once more before the baby arrived. As if he heard me thinking about him—*oops, did I say him?*—he moved a foot or an elbow and jammed me in the side.

"Okay, settle down. We'll have lunch soon. You ready, kiddo?"

As I pulled the yellow purse strap over my shoulder, I heard a nearly inaudible whisper. I froze in the doorway trying to discern where it was coming from. I glanced down at my phone, hoping it was an audio text, but there was nothing on the device. "Who's there?" I called, my voice echoing down the hall of my Victorian home. "Doreen?"

Nobody answered. I walked slowly across the hardwood hallway and stood at the top of the stairs. This was a dangerous place to stand. Isla had tried to kill Detra Ann here in this spot. I did not linger but moved quickly and carefully down the stairs. "Hello?" I called again. The only response was from the curious puppy, who believed I must have had a snack hidden in my hand. His fuzzy round face took the fear out of me, and I smiled at him and inelegantly squatted down to pat his head. "I'll be back. No accidents while I'm gone, okay?" He jumped up and licked me affectionately. I doubted he really understood a word I was saying.

I made the short drive to Detra Ann's house. Well, it was really Detra Ann and Henri's house. The two were nearly inseparable now. It was only a matter of time before they took the big step. I wondered when Henri would pop the question. He sure was taking his time. Detra Ann rarely talked about TD anymore.

Henri, on the other hand, was actively searching for Aleezabeth, as he had promised Lenore he would. He was committed to the task, and he spent quite a bit of time traveling to Louisiana. We'd traveled with him a few times and spent some weekends in New Orleans with him. The food, the people, the beautiful architecture—I could see why so many people loved the place.

I pulled into the driveway of Detra Ann's home and took a deep breath. There were at least a dozen cars, most of which I recognized. It looked like Ashland had made it on time. I smiled, hoping he would be in a good mood. I didn't plan on telling him about my dream, not right now. He had enough to worry about, but I wanted to mention that I had seen Lenore. Maybe he was seeing her too? For some reason, Ashland was always reluctant to talk about the things he saw unless forced to. He was a private man, but he had a warm heart and the most beautiful smile I had ever seen. I was completely in love with him. He had changed my life.

I suddenly remembered the letter from my mother. "Oh, shoot!" I muttered. I had left it on the coffee table at home. I couldn't worry about that right now. Maybe Ashland and I could read it together later.

Grabbing my purse and locking my car, I walked up the brick walkway to the lovely Creole home. Detra Ann had finally bought her own place, and it was chock full of antiques from her store, Cotton City Treasures. She had a flair for displays, and it showed. I rang the bell, and she opened it dramatically. "Should I say surprise?"

I laughed and hugged her. "Not unless you want me to pee on myself."

She laughed too. "I'm just teasing. Come on in here. Look at your belly. That's going to be a big boy! I mean girl. Maybe you'll have one of each."

"Please don't say that," I said, ready to cry at the idea.

She hugged me again, "I'm sorry. I forgot how sensitive preggos can be. I'm sure there is just one baby in there. And he—or she—is perfect."

"Hey, baby!" Ashland walked toward me and scooped me into his arms. "What's this? Are you crying?"

Detra Ann frowned a bit. "It's all my fault, Ash. I'm an insensitive friend. The kind who suggests she's carrying two youngins in there. Just for that, I volunteer to babysit anytime you need me." She kissed my cheek, and I smiled back, wiping away the ridiculous tears. "Y'all come out to the patio when you get ready. Henri thought it would be fun to have this shindig by the pool, and it's only a 'little' hot. He's been cooking, and it's going to be delicious."

"Sounds wonderful. Don't worry about me. I've just got the blues today. And my side is killing me. This kid can kick like you wouldn't believe."

She laughed and said, "I'll get you something to drink and meet you on the patio."

Ashland looked down at me with concern. "What kind of pain are you having? Should we call the doctor?"

With a weak smile and faux confidence, I shook my head. "I don't think it's anything to be concerned about. The last time I mentioned it, Dr. Gilmore said it was probably just my ligaments stretching. I have never heard of contractions in your side, but hey, I'm new to all this childbearing stuff. How did it go today?"

"Nothing I can't manage." He gave a small laugh that didn't sound too cheerful. "Did you hear back from the project manager for the Idlewood house?"

"No. I get the feeling that he wasn't expecting all the red tape. I'm going to back off on the project until after the baby. I'll call him tomorrow and tell him. He'll probably be happy to hear it. Might give him some time to get his act together. Are you sure you're okay?"

He held me in his arms and kissed my forehead. "Stop worrying. Today was just another Monday."

"It's Friday, babe."

"Exactly." He hugged me and whispered, "I love you, Carrie Jo."

"I love you too, Ashland. Please don't make me cry again."

"Ha! How is telling you I love you going to make you cry?"

"You've obviously never been pregnant." I kissed him and released him.

"What's going on that I don't know about?"

With a guilty look I answered, "How did you know?"

"I just know."

"Nothing big, just a dream and a letter. Can we talk about it after the party? Junior or Junior-ette is starving."

He didn't like the compromise, but how could he argue with a hungry child? "All right, but no secrets, remember?" I nodded in agreement. "Oh, wait. I got you this."

He walked to the nearby table and handed me a corsage box with a genuine smile. Ashland was definitely one to shower a girl with flowers. I loved that about him. "How beautiful! Are those Bourbon roses?" I knew they were, but I was enjoying the conversation. This was the first time in recent days that he'd smiled. "Put it on me." I held my arm out, and he slid the fluffy corsage arrangement on my wrist. "I love it, Ashland. It's beautiful."

"Not as beautiful as you, Carrie Jo Stuart."

I rubbed my hands over my belly and turned sideways. "Really? Even with this big belly?"

"Yes, and you get more beautiful every day." I kissed him again, and we walked hand in hand to the patio where our group of friends waited patiently. They applauded as we walked through the open French doors. I smiled at all the faces and accepted hugs from everyone. Chip and Rachel were the first to wish us well. They were on-again, off-again, but I was happy to see them together, at least for the moment. Henri wore one of his many aprons; this one said: *Cooking Up Something Good.* By the smell of it, I knew that was true. Nobody cooked like Henri. And as I predicted, Libby Stevenson, Ashland's attorney, made an appearance. I noticed she recently ditched her long dark hair in favor of a sassy bob. It flattered her angular face. I wondered why she bothered to come when we barely spoke to one another, except in passing. I supposed she came as Ashland's guest. Libby had one of those smiles that never quite made it to her eyes, the kind of smile you couldn't trust.

Whatever, lady, I said to myself. I chose to ignore her but shot Ashland a look. He gazed back at me questioningly. I didn't bother explaining; I shouldn't have to. Less than a minute ago, we were practically making out. Now I wanted to choke him.

Detra Ann spoke up, "Let's get this party started! We're here to welcome Baby Stuart. Thank you all for coming—now let's play some games." For the next 45 minutes we played goofy games and ate crab puffs, gumbo and mini cheesecakes. I laughed about a hundred times and opened a seemingly endless pile of gifts. Jazz played quietly in the background, and Henri surprised me with a beautiful cake.

"Oh my gosh! You bake too?" I dipped my finger into the frosting and tasted it. It was my party, right? Cream cheese frosting so light it tasted like heaven. "When are you going to marry this man? He can do it all."

Everyone got quiet, and I felt embarrassed. I hadn't meant to meddle in their business!

Detra Ann just smiled at me. "Funny you should mention that." She held up her left hand and waved her fingers at me.

"What? Does that ring mean what I think it does?" It was almost as big as mine, and it shone beautifully against her tanned skin. "Oh my gosh! That is beautiful! When? Where?"

Henri smiled and put his arm around Detra Ann. "Last week at the LSU game. I have a friend who works in the booth, and they let me pop the question over the Jumbotron. You should have seen her face."

She squeezed his hand and smiled at me. "Only Henri would do something like that. I thought he was pranking me at first. Until he whipped out this big ol' ring. How could I say no?"

"Why didn't you tell me? Ashland, did you know about this?" He smiled sheepishly and raised his hands as if to say, *I had nothing to do with this.*

"We didn't want to overshadow the shower. This is y'all's party. We planned to have an engagement party after the baby arrives. We'll tell the whole world then."

I felt the tears again for about the fifteenth time that day. This was getting beyond ridiculous. "You guys. That is so wonderful. I am so happy for you both." I hugged Detra Ann, thankful that she had made it through her dark times and found someone as amazing as Henri. She hadn't drunk a drop since Lenore's death, and her antique business was booming. I was so happy for her. She deserved some happiness. Didn't we all?

It appeared that most at the shower had not heard the news, and everyone offered congratulations. "I'm so happy for you both," Libby said in her deep, sultry voice as she hugged Detra Ann halfheartedly. Detra Ann accepted the hug, but I saw her stiffen a bit. She gave Libby an icy smile and moved on to the next person.

I accepted a slice of the cake and sat by the pool listening to Bob Marley and the Wailers and watching my friends. Soon people began to say their goodbyes. Rachel was one of the first. "Sorry, CJ, I have to go. Chip's mother is being a pain in the arse."

"Hey, that's my mom you're talking about," he said defensively.

"And she's a pain in the arse." Rachel rolled her eyes at him and hugged me. "You coming in tomorrow? I have that tree mapped but..." Her voice dropped to a whisper. "I think there's something you should see."

"Really? What is it? Are there pirates in the Stuart tree? I would expect nothing less," I joked.

"It's better to show you than tell you. I promise I'll fill you in tomorrow. I'll be there at 9."

"Call me curious! Of course I'll be there. Thanks, Rachel."

She smiled and left with Chip. I started picking up plates when Detra Ann stopped me. "No, ma'am. No cleaning of any sort. This is your party. Henri and I will take care of this. I think you better figure out where you're going to put all these gifts. Did you drive the BMW?"

"Yep, and Ash drove the Jeep, so we should be okay. I hope. You guys are so generous. I'm going to have to get a bigger house just to have enough room for all this," I said with a laugh.

"No doubt you will." She finished off her glass of punch and observed the remnants of the party. "Wonder why she came?"

"Who's that?" I asked, munching on sugared pecans. She glanced toward Libby. "Oh, her. I don't know. Well, I probably don't want to know."

"Remember when she said, 'I wish you both happiness,' or however she put it?"

"Yes."

"She didn't mean it. My bells went off big time. I mean, why say anything? She's such a liar. Like I said, I don't know why she came. I sure as heck didn't invite her. I don't think she likes anyone here, except Ashland. But then she always was a loner, even in school. Her brother was pretty nice, though."

"Really? I didn't know you guys went to school together. I think we both know why she's here, right?" I rolled my eyes. The young attorney wouldn't be the first woman to have a second thought about my husband. He had practically been a household name before the stranger from Savannah nabbed him. I knew for a fact that half the Historical Society still held a grudge because Ashland married a girl from Georgia and not a "belle from Mobile proper."

"Libby is barking up the wrong tree if she's after Ashland. He's not going to do you like that."

I wiped the sugar from my lips with a yellow napkin. Detra Ann had Ashland's and my initials printed on the napkins, cups and plates. It was a nice touch. I had to remember to keep one for my neglected scrapbook.

As if she heard her name, Libby strolled over to us, her mules slapping on the brick. "Can I help you ladies with something? Need help loading your stuff, Carrie Jo?"

"I think we have it. Thanks."

She stared at me a moment and said, "Well, I guess I'll go, then. Nice party."

As she walked away I felt like a jerk. Not every woman on the planet wanted my husband. Right?

"Nice of you to come, Libby," I called after her. She didn't act like she heard me. Instead, she stood on tiptoe and whispered to Ashland. He leaned down to hear her, and she took advantage of the nearness. Her arms went around his neck, and she hugged him. With her whole body. It was kind of embarrassing. Ash seemed surprised, and he patted her back like she was a child. My raging pregnancy hormones wanted me to slap her into the pool, but I kept my head. *Always listen to your instincts, CJ*, I warned myself.

Detra Ann made a disgusted, snorting sound and yelled, "Ash, we need your help over here."

He said something to Libby, and she left the party. I felt my face flush with embarrassment. Henri sensed the tension and said, "Let's see if we can get this bassinet in the Jeep. If not, I know it will fit in the truck."

"Wonderful party, Detra Ann. Thank you." Avoiding Ashland's eyes, I grabbed a couple bags and headed to the door. I was ready for this day to be over. I felt tired, I had eaten too much, and the green-eyed monster threatened to make an appearance. Detra Ann smiled understandingly and helped me carry the baby's gifts to the car. Thirty minutes later I was headed home with Ashland's Jeep behind me. The way I was feeling, most of this stuff was going to stay in the car overnight. I couldn't imagine hauling it all inside. My puffy feet would never allow that. What made me eat all those crab legs? I felt the sharp pain in my side again, and this time it was so severe I caught my breath.

"Oh God, oh God, oh God," I said as a kind of chant against the pain. Soon it subsided, and I pulled into the driveway. Putting the car in park, I leaned over the steering wheel and waited, hoping it didn't happen again. Ashland seemed oblivious as he juggled pastel-colored gift bags and house keys. When I was sure I was okay, I got out of the car with my purse and a few bags.

Walking up the drive I could feel an oppressive cloud, an unhappy fog unseen by human eye but felt by the spirit. It wasn't a presence, per se, more like bad mojo—or something. I looked up and down the street;

the sun was going down now, and the afternoon traffic had dissipated. Compared to my neighbors' front yard, my flowerbeds looked forlorn and forgotten. Even my newly planted mums had croaked. Why did everything in my yard look dead? I walked up the driveway and almost tripped over a cat. It was the largest black cat I had ever seen outside of the zoo.

"What in the world? Where did you come from?" Like a bolt of lightning, Chunky Boy (that's what I'd decided to call him) ran out of the house after it. "Hey! Come back!"

Ashland was out the door and running past me. "Damn! I'll get him."

I wanted to say something smart like, "Serves you right for leaving the front door wide open," but I kept my mouth shut. I shook my head and headed for the front door when I heard a car slam on its brakes. Chunky Boy yelped, and I dropped my bags. As I ran down to the end of the driveway, I could see Ashland bent over in the street. He picked up Chunky Boy as the driver got out to apologize.

"Oh, I am so sorry. He came out of nowhere. Is he okay?"

Even from this distance, I could see he wasn't. His white fur was covered in blood, and he was clearly lifeless.

For the umpteenth time today I let the tears flow. This time I actually had a reason.

Chapter Three—Rachel

"I've been an unofficial member of the Seven Sisters ghostbusting team from the beginning, but nobody talks much about what happened over there," I complained again. Chip nodded as I continued, "I do believe that Carrie Jo is a dream catcher, though. She's not a huckster. In fact, she's one of the most honest people I know."

His eye roll revealed he had a different opinion. *Gee. That's pretty close-minded of you, Chip.* I decided to change the subject a bit. "What have you heard about the house?"

"I know I'm glad to be out of there, and I can't wait until you've finished up with it completely. Then I won't worry so much. Too many rumors about that place. Did you know it's on the Ghost Hunters website? I think those guys are trying to get in there. You know, to investigate."

"Oh really, nonbeliever? If there's no such thing as ghosts, what would they possibly investigate?"

"I never said there wasn't, but dream catching? I thought that was some Indian myth."

"I think the term you are looking for is Native American," I scolded him. Chip always said the most inappropriate things. He was so unsophisticated. I couldn't believe I'd even agreed to go out with him, much less do anything else with him. I quickly added, "But for your information, I'm not afraid of the house. I like helping out the Historical Society, and it's a big deal for Mobile. Besides, if I didn't manage the tours at

Seven Sisters, who knows what they'd tell the visitors? I wonder about what they teach kids in school these days. Everyone should know the history of the city they live in."

"You sound like an old lady, Rachel Kowalski."

"Me? Because I believe in the unseen, the supernatural? I think you've got that the other way around."

He squinted at me through his glasses as if he didn't quite believe me. The truth was, he was right in a way. I was kind of an old lady. I did worry about everyone and everything. "You didn't answer my question, Chip. Did you see something in the house?"

He said, "I never saw anything, but more than once I felt like someone was watching me. Especially in the Blue Room. Got worse after Hollis Matthews died. It was more of a feeling, that's all. What about you?"

I didn't know if I was ready to tell Chip about my experience. He might think I was losing my mind, as he clearly thought Carrie Jo was a bit loony. He wasn't a deep thinker at all and certainly not spiritual. Once again I wondered how on earth I could be serious about a guy like him. I was totally a spiritual person. I didn't go to church as much as I used to, but I believed in God and the supernatural world. Why did people separate the two? God was a Spirit, right?

I decided to change the subject to a less controversial one. Chip had a short attention span, and he probably wouldn't notice anyway. "Do you believe in curses? Like family curses?"

"Come on, Rachel. You've met my mother," he joked, sipping the remnants of his Starbucks coffee.

"I'm serious. Do you believe in curses, like the Kennedy curse or the Rockefeller curse?"

"Are the Rockefellers cursed?"

I shrugged, aggravated that he was missing the point again. "Just something I heard. So you admit that you believe the Kennedy family is cursed?"

He snorted at the idea. "I didn't say that. I mean, they've had an unusual amount of bad luck. They might be cursed, if that's what you want to call it. I think it's just luck, though. Some families are luckier than others."

"What makes them lucky?"

"I don't know. It's too early in the morning for philosophical discussions, Rachel. You up for dinner tonight? I'm thinking deep-dish pizza from Mushrooms."

"I'm thinking of washing my hair." I opened the car door and grabbed my purse.

"Hey! Don't leave mad. What do you want me to say?" He got out of the car and leaned over the roof of his Volkswagen.

Chip had money. Not Ashland Stuart money, but he came from a wealthy family. He wasn't the handsomest guy on the block, but he wasn't bad-looking either. My biggest complaint was that he lacked imagination. I knew I shouldn't have hooked up with him the first time, let alone again. We were just too different.

"I'm not mad. I just can't make it tonight. I have some major studying to do, but I'll call you. Okay?"

He believed me. I could tell because he beamed from ear to ear. Boy, did he have large ears. *Come on, Rachel! Stop being so damn picky!* He tapped the top of his car happily and watched me unlock the office door before he drove away, completely oblivious to the fact that we were headed for another—permanent—breakup. I would have to deal with that later.

I flicked on the lights, tapped the security code on the alarm pad and made some coffee. CJ never drank coffee anymore, not since her pregnancy, so I made a half a pot. I was firmly committed to drinking every bit of it. I felt tired this morning. Not so much from Chip's snoring but from my constant work on this family tree project for Carrie Jo. I dropped my purse on my desk and went to the conference room, where I arranged the sheets of paper to show CJ my ridiculously detailed research. I looked at it again. Yep, I wasn't imagining things. An entire page of male ancestors dead between the ages of 30 and 40, and most on the lower end of that time frame. I felt a wave of clamminess hit me. *This can't be right*, I'd thought in the beginning. *This has to be some kind of weird coincidence.*

Then I began digging deeper, and that's when things got real hairy. The Stuarts were plagued by freak accidents. For example, one guy got hit by lightning while fishing; another was working on a car, and the dang thing fell on him. Too weird. Things were okay on his mother's side of the tree, but his father's was an entirely different story.

I knew Southern family trees often had tangled roots, but this was crazy. I had traced the Stuarts back to the Cottonwoods—but not Jeremiah Cottonwood. Ashland was related to Isaiah Cottonwood, Jeremiah's brother. In the words of my father, "That puts a whole 'nother spin on that, Sparky." Sparky. Who nicknamed their daughter Sparky? My brother Andy used to tease me and call me "Sparkly" just because he knew it ticked me off. I'd rain down curses on him for all the good it did. Nothing bad ever happened to him. I was lousy at cursing, and I sure as heck knew something about curses. My mother firmly believed in them, as did her sisters, and as a child I tossed salt over my shoulder, avoided crossing streams while wearing a skirt and never, ever stood on a stump—all activities that could have brought down the curses upon myself and my family. Publicly I scoffed at the idea of curses. I often agreed with my childhood friends—curses were superstitious nonsense for scaredy-cats—but after they went home, I crossed my fingers, said the prayers and did whatever it took to keep the curses away.

I knew that what I was looking at was nothing short of a curse. A straight-up curse. I had to tell Carrie Jo. And if she thought I was crazy, well, she wouldn't be the first friend of mine to think so.

"Good morning, Rachel!" she called from the front door. "Coffee smells great! Have a cup for me."

"I will! You need anything?" I called back, delaying a face-to-face meeting for a few more seconds.

"Nope. I'm peachy keen," she said as she poked her head in the doorway. "Oh, cool. Let me go drop this stuff on my desk, and I'll be right back." As she turned to walk away, she groaned and froze, reaching for the doorframe.

"What is it? You okay?" I sprang to my feet, nearly sloshing hot coffee on my starched white blouse.

Her face was pale, which wasn't like CJ at all. All throughout her pregnancy she had amazing skin. Before that she had a nice warm-looking tan. At the moment she appeared near death. "You don't look so hot, girl. Can you walk? I think you should sit down."

"I think you're right," she gasped, holding on to the door like a wavering drunk. Finally, whatever pain had hit her subsided. "Okay, I think I can move now. Darn! My side is killing me."

"You have to go to the doctor, Carrie Jo. You could be in labor."

"Can't be. This pain is in my side. I thought labor pains were in the back or the front."

"I'm not a baby expert, but if I had pain anywhere and I was pregnant, I'd be on my way to the OB-GYN. Can I at least call Ashland?"

"No. Please don't do that. Let's just keep an eye on it. See? It's easing up now." I gave her a disapproving look, and she added, "I'll call my doctor in a few minutes. Promise."

I watched her as she sat at the desk and the color finally returned to her face. "Wow, that was a sharp one. I wonder if I pulled something."

"What have you been doing?"

"Trying to tie my shoes," she said with a laugh. "I'm fine. Stop worrying about me. The pain is gone now. What did you want to show me? I'd be lying if I said I wasn't super-curious."

"I've got everything spread out in the conference room, but I can bring it in here if you like," I offered.

"No. I'm good." She cracked open a water bottle and smiled up at me. Carrie Jo had a beautiful face, a cleft chin, startling green eyes and naturally curly hair. She was a natural beauty, and I often wanted to ask her the brand of coral-colored lipstick she wore. It really played up her light olive skin. You could easily describe her as the girl next door, but she was also usually the funniest girl in the room. I both admired her and felt a bit envious. She'd had some amazing luck in life, including landing the chief historian job at Seven Sisters. Of course, her bestie had almost killed her, and quite a few of her friends had died. I suddenly felt ashamed for the envy.

"Great. Whenever you're ready, just come to the conference room."

"Okay, be there in a second."

After a few minutes she joined me and sat next to me, looking over the sheaves of paper. "Beautiful work, Rachel. How's it going in school? Ready to graduate?"

"Dear Lord, yes. Did you get the graduation invitation?"

"Yes! And if I'm not having a baby, I'll be there." She laughed and made a face that let me know she was ready to get on with the whole childbirth experience. I didn't blame her. She was all baby now. Her arms and legs were much thinner than before, and it seemed like the baby was stealing all her nutrients. But then again, what did I know?

With a smile I handed her the first piece of paper. I used the Alari software to create the family tree. I thought it would be easy enough, but filling in the slots on the electronic tree had been anything but. Alari verified each entry, and when it couldn't find source records it forced the user to provide verification via GEDCOM, Rootsweb or one of the dozens of other genealogical sites. I sat beside her and allowed her to look through the papers before I spoke up.

"So this is the completed version. It took me about forty hours of research to find all the connections."

"Oh no. I had no idea I was asking you to work that many hours. I expect to compensate you, Rachel. This is wonderful work."

I shook my head. "No way. This is my baby gift. Remember? As you can see, Ashland comes from a long line of tangled relations." I smiled tentatively at her. Maybe I shouldn't tell her anything. She had enough going on now. What with the pain and the baby.

"Hey, what's the deal? Is this right?"

I peeked at the paper she was holding. It was the information about Isaiah Cottonwood and his connection to Ashland. "Yep, it's right."

"So Ashland is not a direct descendant of Jeremiah Cottonwood? I can't say I'm disappointed. I've never heard of Isaiah. Or maybe I have, but I just don't remember him."

"He never came up in our previous research, Carrie Jo. Funny thing is, Ashland is both a direct descendant of the Cottonwoods and a cousin to the Beaumonts. See here? In 1870, Dara Beaumont married this guy, and that's the cousin. Not unusual when families stick close to home. Apparently in this family group, people kind of hung around and didn't move away when they got older. Except Calpurnia, but she didn't have much choice. See?" I pointed to another section of the genealogy.

"I wonder what this will mean for his estate."

"I'm not sure, CJ."

"Here's something even more surprising. There is a codicil to Jeremiah's will."

"Yes, I heard about that."

"You knew?" I asked, surprised.

Her cheeks went pink. "Not until recently."

"Here is a copy of it that I made from the archives downtown. It clearly transfers all property rights to Isaiah. Jeremiah must have been quite a jerk. This codicil was created just a month before he died, and with it he basically took the family fortune away from his daughters and his in-laws and gave it to his brother. Which sucks since most of the money probably belonged to the Beaumonts originally."

"That does suck," Carrie Jo added, still staring at the pages. I promised myself I wouldn't say a word unless she did. The idea of talking about a curse seemed ridiculous to me now. Except for the evidence. I handed her a copy of the spreadsheet that displayed the birth dates, death dates and ages of the deceased. Maybe she would notice it herself. She said, "Good work, Rachel." She scanned the printed sheet down to the bottom.

Carrie Jo stared at Ashland's name for a second and then scanned back up. She saw it too! With wide eyes she looked at me. "And you are sure about these ages?"

"I doubled-checked everything, CJ. It's all accurate. I even had Chip look at it with me. You know he's got a photographic memory."

Carrie Jo didn't say much but kept staring at the page. "Why so young? I mean, I know people back then didn't live as long as we do, but 35 seems very young to die. And it's men only? How many generations does this phenomenon go back?"

"Near as I can tell, right around the time of the codicil. Isaiah's sons, Jacob and Christian, died at age 31 and 34, respectively, but his two daughters both lived into their sixties. Next generation, these three men, all dead before 35. And it goes on until today."

"And Ashland is about to have a birthday." I could hear the fear in her voice.

"I'm sure it's nothing, Carrie Jo. I mean, I noticed it too, but what could it mean? The Cottonwood line has had some bad luck, but a lot of families experience tragedy. Try not to worry about this." I regretted pointing this out; the look on her face said it all. "Don't obsess over this stuff. It's nothing to worry about." *Or nothing you can do anything about, anyway.*

She didn't look at me but kept staring at the papers. She pulled her phone out of her purse. "Maybe not, but I know someone who can tell me what I'm looking at—I hope." I watched her dial the number, and my heart beat faster. "Hey, Henri? You got a minute? I'd like to come see you. I need your opinion on something. Sure, I can be there in a few minutes. Yes, breakfast sounds great. No, Ashland isn't with me. Just Rachel. Great. We'll be there in 15."

She put the phone down and stared at the papers again. I was dying to ask so I did, "How can Henri help?"

"He's a bit of a spiritualist. He knows a thing or two about supernatural subjects. You up for some pancakes? He's got extra."

Happy to finally be included in something beyond answering phones and creating reports, I nodded with a smile.

"Grab your purse and let's go. We need to bring these papers too."

"I've got these. You get your purse. I'll drive, CJ."

"I'll let you." As I slid the papers into the envelope, a shadow crossed the window outside. The sky suddenly seemed darker. Was there a storm brewing? This changeable weather was one of the things I disliked the most about Mobile. You could be lying out in the sun in the backyard one minute and getting drenched the next. A flash of lightning popped across the distant sky. It came from the direction of the harbor.

Yep. There was definitely a storm brewing.

But what kind?

Chapter Four—Carrie Jo

The two of us didn't talk much as we drove to Henri's. I could tell Rachel wanted to say something to comfort me, but what could she say? Suddenly everything I'd been through the past few days made sense. The arguments, the bad luck, the feeling of oppression. Sounded like a curse to me, but I was no expert.

Henri now lived in the apartment over Detra Ann's antique store, but honestly that wasn't much of a move. Cotton City Treasures was only two streets over from his old digs. And it wasn't a permanent move, now that they were getting married. I loved his apartment, though. It was in an old building with fabulous gargoyles perched at the corners of the roof. A rarity in Mobile. There weren't many such objects in the downtown area. There was an interesting pyramid building with two sphinxes at the door. Some kind of Masonic lodge, probably. I'd never asked about it, but it was on my to-do list. If I ever had the time.

And if I could ever get the supernatural stuff cleared away. Between the ghosts, the dreams and the specter of Death, I'd been a little busy. Now I suspected that something else hung over us, over Ashland and our child. Maybe that was why I had been so resistant to the idea of having a son. Did I somehow psychically know that the Cottonwood boys were cursed? I needed to show the evidence to Henri and let him tell me what he thought. He came from a family who understood curses and hexes, as he had related to us many times.

I did the math while Rachel drove. Two men in that generation, then three, then two, then four more. I couldn't remember the second page, but I would never forget seeing Ashland's name at the bottom. No way could I tell him about this.

"Oh my God!" I said as a flock of crows hovered in front of our car. They hung in the air for a moment, then flapped their wings and flew away. "Holy smokes! What was that about?"

"I...have...no...idea," Rachel said slowly. She was gripping the steering wheel so tightly her knuckles were white.

We pulled in front of the antique store, and I waved at Detra Ann as I got out of the car. I looked over my shoulder to make sure the evil birds weren't stalking me. She waved back but didn't stop to chat. An excited customer was purchasing a blue and white tray and asking the pretty ponytailed blonde a bunch of questions about other items in the shop. I pointed to the stairs, and she nodded at me as the breathless patron kept up with her queries.

I didn't know how Detra Ann worked with the public, but she loved it. It took someone special to take a public relations degree and use that to run an antiques shop. One of the things I loved about her new business was that every item came with a story. Not just word of mouth, either. No, Detra Ann had hidden talents. She wrote what she knew about each item and made sure the new owner got a copy of her story. The community and its visitors loved her place. *It's like she was born for this.*

We walked up the narrow stairs to the apartment and opened the glass door that led to Henri's loft. After Lenore died, he had sold his house and moved in here instead. I didn't blame him. It was a gorgeous open space with warm painted walls and to-die-for fixtures and extras.

"So what's up, ladies?" Henri tossed off his apron, which read: *Boo-yah.* "Who wants some pancakes? I made enough for a small army—I had a feeling I'd have guests this morning." He rubbed his hands together as he served us with gusto. He was obviously proud of both his premonition and his pancakes. I took a bite. He had reason to be.

"I'll take a few of these. As always, it smells like heaven in here."

"You want the syrup warmed?"

"Whatever is easiest, Henri. Thanks for this." Rachel blushed as he handed her a plate of hot pancakes. I smiled a bit. I never knew Rachel had a crush on Henri, but then again I had been kind of self-involved for the past few months. I knew she liked Detra Ann, though, so I didn't worry about any shenanigans there.

After he poured the juice and set everything on the table, I handed him the stack of papers. "Take a look at this and let me know what you think."

With a curious look he accepted the envelope and put on a pair of gold-rimmed glasses.

"Glasses, huh?"

"No jokes, CJ. My eyes may be old, but I'm not."

I chuckled and covered my mouth with my hand as I chewed a delicious bite of pancake. I was hungrier than I thought. And to think, I'd walked away from Doreen's omelet this morning. But then again, our housekeeper's cooking didn't stack up against Henri's. I'd often told him he needed to open a restaurant. So far, I hadn't convinced him.

"Okay, what am I looking at?" He stared at the papers and looked up at the light. "Did it just get dark outside? The news didn't say anything about bad weather this morning. That storm is way off the coast." He hopped up and flipped the light switch, and the beautiful fleur-de-lis embellished chandelier filled the dining room with warm light.

"What storm?" Rachel asked.

"Looks like we have a late tropical storm brewing off the coast, but it's pretty far away." He went to the window and looked outside. It had gotten dark quickly, first at the office and now here. As the old folks used to say, it "looked like the bottom would fall out of the sky" any minute.

I loved Henri's place. It had so much New Orleans flair; cool photos from his time there covered the living room walls. A collection of fleur-de-lis candle holders rested on a side table. One of the walls in the living room was painted a dark red, and an elegant gold-rimmed mirror hung in the center of it.

He slid the papers out of the envelope and shuffled through them quickly before he began intently studying them. He didn't ask me what to look for, and I could tell when he spotted it. "So he has a birthday in about a month?"

I nodded, wiping my mouth with the linen napkin and pushing the plate to the side. It was wonderful, but I'd lost my appetite again. "Do you think it's possible that we—that we're…"

"Cursed?" Rachel answered for me.

"Yeah, what she said." If I didn't say the word, then we wouldn't be, right?

"Let's look at the facts, and then we'll look at the rest. According to this, every man in Ashland's family tree—in this particular line of ancestors, anyway—has died at an early age. From these notations about the causes of death, it looks like a string of accidents."

"Some. I can't be sure about a few of the others, so I left question marks beside their names. Even if you assumed that those men died of natural causes, that's still a lot of early deaths." Rachel added in a serious voice, "Men usually died around age 55 to 60 during the early to mid-1800s. There's definitely a trend of men dying young in that particular family."

"No doubt there is. How old is Ashland now?"

"He'll be thirty. We've joked about the baby coming on his birthday. And that's another thing—what about the baby? What if I have a boy? What will that mean?"

"Hold up, let's not jump to any conclusions." Just then a bolt of lightning cracked through the sky and illuminated our faces in blue light. I winced at the closeness of it. The lights flickered, but the power didn't go out. I heard the shop door ring downstairs; we'd left Henri's door ajar on accident. I heard footsteps coming up the stairs. Feeling creeped out about curses, I turned to look and was relieved to see it was Detra Ann.

You are being ridiculous, CJ. All the ghosts have settled down. You're just looking for trouble. If you're not careful, you'll find it.

Detra Ann slid her arms around my neck and hugged me. I needed all the hugs I could get right now. I squeezed her back, and she grabbed a plate. "I'm stealing some breakfast, but help me keep an ear out for customers. I've got the buzzer set. It sure got dark outside, didn't it? I might have to bring my antiques table inside, Henri. I think it's going to flood any minute. What are y'all up to?"

It was just like Detra Ann to talk in a constant stream of consciousness. She plopped down in the empty chair with her plate and dug into the pancakes.

"We've found something weird. It has to do with Ashland. Have you ever heard about a, well, I guess the thing you could call it is a..." Why was this so difficult to say?

"A curse, she's talking about a curse." Henri filled in the blank this time.

"What kind of curse? Like a hex or something?"

"No. More like a family curse," Rachel said. "All of Ashland's male relatives from the Cottonwood line died early deaths. We're just concerned about him since his birthday is around the corner."

"So you think Ashland is cursed? What would make you say that?" She put her fork down and stared at the three of us.

Henri handed her the family tree, and as she flipped through it he questioned me, "What's been going on? He mentioned he's had some legal troubles recently. What else is happening?"

"I don't know. What am I supposed to be looking for?"

Rachel raised her hand. "Um, I can answer that. The women in my family are experts on curses."

"Oh, so like they're witches?" Detra Ann asked innocently between drinking orange juice and nibbling on her pancakes.

"Lord, don't tell them that. No, they aren't witches at all. They're just very superstitious. My mother and her four sisters break curses all the time. They can spot them a mile away too." She snapped her fingers. "I am sure they would be able to tell if you or Mr. Stuart had one!"

"Whoa, let's not get ahead of ourselves here. We don't know if he's—if we're…"

"Cursed?" Detra Ann finished for me.

"Well if you believe in curses—and I've always been taught that you have to believe in them for them to work—a number of things can cause them," Henri began to explain.

"Not to contradict my elders," Rachel said with a smile, "but that's not entirely true."

Henri leaned back in his chair and drank his coffee as another pop of lightning came close to the shop. "What can you tell us about curses, Rachel?"

"Well, they manifest differently, and they can fall on individuals and families gradually. The way I understand it, curses work the opposite of a blessing. You know, when you say a blessing over food or you bless someone for some special reason?"

"Or say, 'Bless her heart'?" Detra Ann joked, obviously trying to lighten the mood.

"Not quite like that, no. Bad stuff happens to people all the time, but when it hits you nonstop it might just be a curse. A curse is basically negative energy that gets bound to a person for some supernatural reason. For example, in our family, we believe that if you steal, you've put yourself under a curse. Negative acts bring curses. Sometimes someone can send a curse to you, but you would have to do them wrong in a major way for them to be able to curse an entire family for generations. I'm talking about a serious curse here."

"What other evidence do you have to support the idea that Ashland might be cursed?" I could tell by her tone that Detra Ann wasn't convinced, and I was glad for that. I still couldn't even say the word.

"You know what? We have had some issues lately. He's had lawsuit after lawsuit, things keep breaking around the house, we argue all the time. It's like we're in this funk and can't get out of it."

Nobody spoke for a minute, and then Henri asked, "What about animals? Any weird encounters?"

"On the way here, a flock of crows nearly caused us to have an accident." Rachel's voice sounded even quieter now, and I shivered when I saw her spill salt in her hand and toss it over her shoulder.

I cleared my throat and made a confession. "That's not all. Some stray cat on our street lured our puppy into the road, and he got hit by a car. He died." I chewed on my lip for a second while my friends stared at me wide-eyed. "Also, things keep coming up missing, like we've got a thieving gremlin in the house. I just chalked it up to me being absentminded because of the pregnancy, but I'm thinking it's something else now. Can this be possible? I mean, everyone here knows that the supernatural world exists, but this kind of thing…a…"

"Curse, Carrie Jo. It's a curse. Saying it won't make you more cursed, I promise." Rachel patted my hand.

"Yeah, well, curses. That's a whole other ballgame. This can't be right."

"But that's the thing about a curse. It's not in your face. It's sneaky. Most people don't even seem to notice they are under one."

"I agree with Rachel. If we can do something to prevent it, break it, we should. If his birthday goes by and nothing happens, then we know we're good."

"Until next year," Rachel mumbled.

"So I'll just stress out for the next ten years every time he has a birthday? No. If Ashland is cursed, I want to break it, right now—today! It's not just Ashland. It's the baby too, if we're having a boy. And there's another thing." I turned to Henri, who watched me intently with his warm dark eyes. "I saw Lenore, Henri. She was speaking, trying so hard to tell me something, but I couldn't understand her. It was a word."

"If Lenore is involved, then the chances that something is wrong have increased dramatically. She would want to help, no matter where she was. No clue at all what she was trying to say?"

I took a sip of milk and shook my head. "I had a dream and was about to wake up. That's when she came, at that in-between place. I can't explain it any better than that. I could see her pretty clearly, but it sounded like she was trying to talk underwater. Then she was gone and I was awake. It was so fast I couldn't work out what she said."

Detra Ann reached across the table and grabbed my hand. "Hey. We're with you. We all love you and Ashland. If there's a curse, we'll figure out how to break it. But…I have to say this. I think it's a good idea to keep this to ourselves for now. No need to freak him out. We all know how much he hates this kind of stuff. You said yourself, he's been under quite a bit of stress recently."

Rachel's forehead wrinkled with concern. "What? If I was cursed, I would want to know it. I know I'm not as close to Ashland as you guys are, but I wish you'd reconsider that."

I looked from one face to the other, not sure what to say. "I think Detra Ann is right. For now—just for now, Rachel—we don't say anything to Ash. But didn't you say that for a generational curse to work it had to be sent by someone who was done wrong in a big way?"

"Yes, that's what I understand. Let me check with my mom, though. Like I said, she and my aunts are the expert on curses."

Henri put the papers back in the envelope and handed them to me. "While she does that, I'll check with a friend in New Orleans. He's a pastor there. Whenever I need prayer, he's the guy I call on. Let's get him praying over this situation. Maybe he can get some spiritual insight into what we're dealing with. I think the big question is who put this curse on Ashland's ancestors, and how do we break it? It's going to be difficult to make things right if the curser has been dead for over a hundred years."

For some reason I just had to laugh. Like the old-timers said, "You either laugh or cry." Everyone looked at me like I was sure-enough, put-her-in-the-loony-bin crazy. "I don't mean to laugh. I swear. It's just what you said." I stifled more laughter. "About the curser being dead. I mean, these Cottonwoods and Beaumonts don't die. I don't know why you're worried about that." Then the tears came, and Detra Ann put her arms around me. I cried on her shoulder, feeling more tired than I had ever felt in my life.

She whispered kindly to me, "It's going to be fine, CJ. I promise you, I'll stick close to Ashland. He'll think we're joined at the hip. Maybe I'll start by meeting him for lunch today. Keep an eye on him. I can call Cathy in to work the shop for me."

I gave a sigh of relief. Not because I had all the answers. Quite the opposite. I had a bunch of questions. But at least I had my friends. We had friends.

"That leaves me. I'll do the one thing I know I can do." My friends knew what I meant. I'd be dreaming, but with a purpose this time. It had been a while since I pursued the past through the dream world. I'd had plenty of dreams, but those came naturally and were less taxing than dreaming with a purpose. I didn't mention what I had seen about Olivia and Isla. That might not be relevant...oh, who was I kidding? I was pretty sure the evil blonde cherub would be involved somehow. But why bring up Isla to Detra Ann? The dead girl had tried to kill her!

It was always risky going back to Seven Sisters, but now that the spirits had settled down, I was sure it wouldn't be so dangerous.

I hoped.

Chapter Five—Karah

Sitting on the worn blue quilt, I shook my blue silk purse and listened to the sound of the last of my coins. Hoping it was more than it sounded, I loosened the cord and dumped the coins on the bed. This wasn't enough to make it through the week, much less another month in Mobile. Out of sheer embarrassment I had refused to stay with Delilah, but my pride had cost me. I was no charity case, and I refused to allow Jackson to cover the expense of my continued stay here at the boarding house. I had to make plans for my future, but the truth was I had nowhere to go. Mother had sold our home in Virginia, and God only knew what she did with the money. Docie probably knew, but she would never tell me. She was always Mother's creature, although I suspected she had abandoned her and taken Mother's meager supply with her.

This trip had cost me all my savings, but it cost me even more than that. I had been spent emotionally in ways I had not expected. Why had I come to Mobile? Why had I trusted Mother? The small stipend she gave me had long since disappeared, and I had no other means of support. When Mother sent me to Seven Sisters, she assured me that all would be well. Ah, she excelled at lying, and I excelled at believing her. But no more.

She had made claiming my inheritance sound like a mere formality. She had assured me that my father had made provision for me and that local society would not question my parentage. "They will see your beauty and know right away that you are a Cottonwood. No, *the* Cottonwood." But society had not accepted me at all, and neither had my father's family; none had accepted my invitations to visit me at Seven Sisters. I had received a few letters from an uncle I did not know, but I had not been allowed to read them. Docie snatched them up and kept them secreted away until Mother arrived.

"You let your mother deal with this man," she warned me as tersely as possible.

All I had to do was wait for her, care for the house and most importantly of all—find the Beaumont treasure.

But she had been wrong, and no treasure had yet been found. Jackson informed me that the will was very specific and that I needed proof that I was who I claimed to be. I had no proof, only the word of my mother. I wrote her and informed her of the many challenges I faced in Mobile. She wrote me back, but it was only one line:

I will succeed. I am on the way.

I received no more letters, but a short time later Docie returned. She had hard eyes and a cruel grip, which she did not mind applying to my young wrists. Easy enough to hide the bruises. "Wear gloves, Karah," my mother would tell me. She did not care one whit what Docie did to me.

It wasn't until I was almost ten that I understood that Mother went mad sometimes. During those dark times I would be sent away to a nearby girls' home until she recovered. I had a few happy times, though. Especially when Captain Garrett came to us. He insisted that I call him Uncle David, which I liked. I much preferred pretending he was my father, but from my earliest age Mother made sure I knew he was not.

"You are a Cottonwood, my dove. That is much better than being a Garrett." I hated seeing the hurt on the captain's face, but I did not dare argue with her. How I missed the captain! He brought joy into my dim life for a time, and when he left us for good, darkness descended.

I had heard it said that Mother had been a great actress in her prime, but she did not speak of it much anymore. How I loved seeing her standing in the spotlight, although I had to witness her performances in secret. "Theaters are for mature minds," she would say before she stepped into the carriage and disappeared into the night with a wave or a scowl. Thankfully Docie would leave with her and I would be alone.

Occasionally, I would steal into Mother's rooms for a while and read her plays. If the trunks were left open, and they rarely were, I would grab a gown and hold it up to my small body pretending that I was my beautiful mother. Of course I had to be careful to put the dresses back the way I found them.

Once, while we traveled through Virginia, I did sneak into a theater to see her. It wasn't hard to do. We traveled with a company of actors through a string of Virginia cities, and the hotels were often very near the theaters. I crept out at quite a few of them; often I pretended that I had to deliver something to Isla Garrett, as she sometimes called herself. The usher let me pass, but I never made it to the dressing room. I hung back in the shadows of the stage and chewed on my fingernail or a stolen apple as I waited for the play to begin. It was like watching someone I did not know. She wholly transformed herself each night and became whomever she pretended to be. I could not believe this breathtaking, living doll was my own mother. She was a magical creature full of light and laughter. It was almost as if she could change her features, her voice, her body shape. She could have played Hamlet himself if she had taken a mind to.

That seemed a hundred years ago; now she sat in a mental asylum awaiting trial for attempted murder. I could hardly believe it!

The weeks went by and shamefully I had not seen her once. How could I, after what she tried to do? That did not stop Docie from coming to see me. She demanded that I attend my mother, defend her, help her in some way. I refused. I did not know the devil she had become.

But I had found a friend in Adam Iverson. One early evening, when I ventured out long enough to find needed toiletries, I ran into him on the sidewalk outside the boarding house. He was kind to me and offered to help me with my packages. I refused, of course, but he begged to take me to dinner. Overwhelmed with loneliness I accompanied him to a small dining room on the outskirts of town. He was flirtatious, as he had always been, but not too inappropriate. The following day he left a bouquet of flowers for me at the front desk, and I had spent much time with him since that first dinner. I had other visitors too. Jackson came a few times. He carefully let me know that it was Delilah who sent him. It was clear to me that she was the object of his true affection. I cared not, for I had my eye on Adam. He was strong, clever with his ideas and amiable enough. At least for a little while.

But I did miss Delilah, and I was happy to hear that she got stronger every day. The slice on her leg had become infected, but she had recovered and was apparently anxious to see me. I couldn't face her either. I made my apologies to the attorney and promised I would visit my cousin soon. I did not bother to inquire about my own legal status. How could I make a claim now when my only true witness to my parentage had gone mad?

Imagine my surprise when Stokes showed up at my door. My mother had been released and was residing again at Seven Sisters, he told me in his loud, deep voice. Not only that, but a relative of mine, a Mrs. Torrence, requested my presence at the house. I considered calling Mr. Keene, as he had been gone only a few minutes, but I felt better about making this trip by myself. I left a message for Adam with Mrs. Shields, my landlady. I asked him to wait for my return at his shop. I would come see him soon. How could I involve any more innocent people in what could only be considered my family's madness?

Curious now, I collected my purse and followed Stokes to the carriage that would take me to the grand old house. Of course I knew the name, Olivia Torrence. She was Isla's mother and my grandmother, but I had no knowledge of her involvement in our lives at any point up until now, and so naturally I was suspicious of her. If I learned anything from my mother, it was to be suspicious and to question the motives of everyone around me. Especially my mother's.

As the carriage pulled into the long driveway of Seven Sisters, I did not experience the wonder and happiness that I had the first time I made this journey. The white columns used to rise up like a welcoming temple in the promised land. Now the massive home seemed more like a mausoleum, for there was no one about. A massive mausoleum full of secrets and lies. There were only a few lights burning in the windows this evening. The dim light added to the solemnity I already felt. Whatever could Mrs. Torrence want with me? She had cast off my mother as a child; I could not hope for better, could I? Then the likely truth occurred to me: she wanted what all Beaumonts wanted—the return of their fortune. Like my mother, Mrs. Torrence pinned all her hopes on me to be the one who brought her the reward. I would disappoint her too because I knew nothing at all and had found nothing at all. Whatever treasure had been there, it was long gone now. Or hidden so carefully in the house or grounds that it would take ten lifetimes to recover it.

To continue to seek it would be madness.

I made my way into the house cautiously, as if someone or something would jump out at me any moment. I fully understood the phrase "on pins and needles" as I made my way from the open foyer to the ladies' parlor. The first thing I saw was the pale face of my mother as she sailed toward me with a smile.

"Mother? Why are you here?"

Ignoring my question, she said gaily, "Here is my lovely daughter, Aunt."

I raised my eyebrows at both her greeting and her address of "Aunt." I had always thought Olivia to be my grandmother, not my great-aunt. While my mother was animated and showering me with forced affection, the older woman hardly moved. She sat like a thin, tall statue in the largest chair in the ladies' parlor.

"Karah, this is your aunt and mine, Olivia Torrence."

"How did you get out, Mother? I thought you were to stand trial for what you did to us?" I didn't bother with the formalities. We were not a formal family.

"Yes, and little you did to help me! Imagine not helping your mother when she needed you the most! I sat in that jail with all those other women! No family. No friends. Barely any food at all. Do you know what I went through? The guards mistreated me—of course, men only want one thing. That's all they think about. Like your father! You ungrateful—"

Mrs. Torrence exclaimed, "Isla! That is enough! Sit down before I have Stokes tie you to a chair and gag you. You will contain yourself, or you can return to Holy Angels Sanitarium. Now, Miss Cottonwood, please have a seat here at the table."

I cast an angry look at my mother but took the seat across from her. How different the two women were in spirit, though they were very much alike in physical appearance. Olivia stood a near head taller than Mother. That I could tell even though she had not yet stood. They had similar etched features, like two lovely porcelain dolls, but they were made of ice, not porcelain. Olivia dressed more demurely than Isla, but she was older. Old enough to be Isla's mother. I wondered again how this family tree ran.

"You must have many questions for me, and I certainly have some for you."

I nodded but kept my mouth shut. It seemed better to collect information than share it, and I could do that only if I kept quiet. "Are you the daughter of Jeremiah Cottonwood?" Olivia asked.

"I have been told all my life that I am." I held my head high and stared daggers at my mother.

"You have the look of the Cottonwoods. The wide mouth, the colorful cheeks. I would say that you could be."

"She most certainly is! Even Jeremiah acknowledged her."

"Yes, but the courts haven't, have they? And your recent performance makes it less likely that they will. However, all is not lost yet."

"Truly? Tell us, Aunt. What do you have planned?" Isla smiled broadly as if she had been given a long-awaited gift.

"I do not need your help in establishing Karah. You leave that to me."

"She is my daughter!"

"Unfortunately for her. But she is not yours to worry over anymore, Isla. She is my ward and in my care until she is established. The only thing you can bring her is shame and notoriety. Imagine working as an actress! What were you thinking?"

Isla stood up and slung the chair back. It made a scraping sound as it slid across the floor. "I did what I had to do! You cannot keep me from my only child."

Without standing or arguing, Aunt Olivia rang the bell beside her. Stokes came immediately. "Please escort my niece to her room and make sure she stays there until I summon her," Aunt Olivia said coolly.

"You cannot imprison me, Olivia! I will not have it."

"You have nothing to say about it. Now go peaceably, or Stokes can pick you up and carry you. Whichever you prefer." With an angry scowl, Isla did as she was told. It was likely the first time in her life she had obeyed anyone. It was certainly the first time I had ever witnessed such a thing. Even Uncle David had not been able to command such obedience. I immediately feared and liked my great-aunt.

"Will you imprison me as well?"

Olivia poured me a cup of tea and slid it to me. "Come. Let us put the knives away. As the daughter of a madwoman, you will appreciate the honest truth."

I sipped my tea nervously and said, "If you knew she was mad, why did you leave me with her? Why have I never met you, Aunt Olivia?"

She toyed with a sugar cube as if she weren't sure what to say to me. With slender fingers she tossed the cube into the lukewarm tea and stirred it with a golden spoon. "She was Louis' daughter. Who was I to interfere? If he wanted to leave her in a girls' home or send her overseas, I had nothing to do with it. If it pleased him to tell everyone that she was my bastard daughter, then that was fine too. Nobody who knew me believed his stories. Louis was one to tell tales. He and Christine were both such dreamers. I was the practical one. I married a practical man and have lived a very respectable life, all told. It wasn't until I learned what Louis had done with our fortunes that I decided I must do something."

"I see. You gave no thought for me at all until your fortune became involved…"

"This will be the last time I remind you, put the knives away, girl. You are no match for me, and I will not be swayed by your insults. Do nothing foolish; I am the only one who can help you."

"Really? You want to help me now?" I swallowed the anger and resentment that began to brew within me. "How do you propose to do that?"

She leaned back in her chair and closed her eyes for a moment. I watched and waited to see what would happen next.

"When I met my husband, Louis practically disowned me. If it weren't for our mother, God rest her soul, I am sure he would have. You see, he was the son, the heir to all our fortunes, but he was not a wise man. He arranged for Christine to marry Jeremiah, knowing full well that she loved another."

"The doctor?"

"I see you know your family history. Yes, the doctor."
She opened her eyes and smiled, but not at me. She was
thinking about something. "Louis loved Christine and
me, but he was easily influenced. He wouldn't think
twice if he needed to use you for something. And as we
all loved him so much, we tolerated him."

"Why are you telling me this?" I asked her.

She seemed not to hear me. She stood, walked to the
French door and stared out of it. "He cared for
Jeremiah, in his way, but he did not love him the way
Jeremiah wanted him to. So he gave Jeremiah the next
best thing. He gave him Christine. I told our mother all
about it. I begged her to stop the marriage, to save
Christine, but she believed Louis. Louis thought it
would be a good match. The two most powerful houses
together, joining their bloodlines and their wealth to
establish a dynasty. He had such dreams and hopes."

"But Jeremiah didn't love Christine. He loved Louis.
He treated her badly and swore at her in my presence.
My own husband tried to stop the marriage, but to no
avail. I knew nothing but disaster would come of it."
She sat down again. Sitting up straight, her arms on the
armrests, she looked like a beautiful queen, a tired old
queen reflecting on her life on the last day of it. "Then
the gossipers came. Jeremiah was burning through the
money. He made poor investments, spent money on
new slaves, the kind he liked, and God knows what else.
He was a devil of a man.

"At that time, I went to Isaiah, Jeremiah's brother, and
pleaded with him to intercede. I told him about the love
his brother had for Louis. I told him Jeremiah would

ruin us both, but he laughed in my face. He told me to stop interfering in my sister's marriage. If she wasn't complaining, who was I to do so? I almost believed him, but I went to Christine. She confessed to me her love for Hoyt Page. What could I do? Mother died, and there was no one left who could influence Louis to do what was right. Soon he began traveling to New Orleans, and for a time, I thought he fell in love. Unfortunately, she was a whore. Imagine how I greeted her when he brought her to our family home. I turned her out before she could put her feet up. How he hated me for that!"

She sighed sadly and straightened her dress. "After that, he had nothing for me. No more brotherly love. We were estranged. I stayed out of his business and tried my best to salvage whatever was left of the family fortune. Then your mother came here. She made things worse. She got pregnant with you and complicated things even more. Somewhere, she says, there is a codicil that names you as sole heir to Seven Sisters and the other Cottonwood properties. Without it, everything will go to Isaiah, Jeremiah's hateful brother. Now my sister is dead, my brother is dead, and I am left to clean this mess up! How cruel fate can be!"

She slammed her fists down on the table, causing the candles to flicker in their heavy brass holders. It was the most emotional thing I had seen her do.

"Fortunately, niece, my husband has a great amount of influence in the government of Alabama. One stroke of his pen, and he can make you legitimate. You will inherit Seven Sisters, as the late Mr. Cottonwood wished. You will have your own money, so you can live comfortably. And best of all, your mother will not be around to steal it from you. I plan on taking her back to north Alabama when I leave, provided you agree to my terms."

My mind swam at what she offered me. I would be legitimate—at least legally. I could be free from my mother's shadow and her ever-reaching hands. I knew there must be a catch.

"Why would you do this for me? I know there is a reason. Please do me the courtesy of telling me what that reason is, madam. I deserve to know the truth."

"You will allow my investigators to locate my missing property. If they are unable to do so, you will sell whatever lands and assets you possess to provide me with the return of the Beaumont money. Minus this house, of course. I would not dream of claiming your family home. And one last thing. You will testify against Miss Page and refuse to recognize her as your relative. Neither she nor her sister, if she should reappear later, will have any claim on this place or the Beaumont fortune."

I shot to my feet, boiling with anger. How dare she demand anything at all! Of all my so-called family, only Delilah had been kind to me. In fact, she loved me. That much I knew, even though I had not been as kind to her recently. I felt even more ashamed that I had not seen her or spoken to her in weeks. "You cannot demand such a thing. Why would I renounce the only family I have for your gain? You ask too much. I am nothing without loyalty."

Olivia rose to her feet, but her voice stayed calm and cool. "If you want my assistance, those are the terms. I have everything I need with me. We can visit the courthouse to see the judge whenever you like. Think what this could mean for you, girl. Think about yourself for a change. I will give you a day to think about it. If you refuse, then you will never see me again. And you will have no one to support you."

How was it that I could be denied love so frequently? Was I not worthy of love? I had not chosen to be born, and I had not chosen my parents. Yet, everyone rejected me again and again. Except Delilah. She alone had accepted me. Without her, I would have no family at all. I had not wanted this fortune, and I was not willing to pay the price that my mother and aunt apparently were. Such beauty. Such cold hearts.

"I am glad to hear that you are taking my mother with you. I have long since known that she needed the care of someone skilled at managing her. I do hope you know what you are undertaking. As far as this house goes, I have no attachment to it. I do not care if you burn it to the ground. And as for my cousin, I will not deny her, either privately or publicly. She is the only family I have, and I will not disown her, even if it means I will be penniless. I would like to say it was pleasant to meet you, but it hasn't been. Good day to you, Aunt Olivia. You promised me I would not see you again—it is a promise I hope you keep." I swung my skirts out from under the table and walked toward the door.

"Where are you going? Do you intend to walk back to the boarding house? How long do you think you will live on the change you have in that purse? I suppose you could earn a living on your back. Maybe that is a talent your mother can teach you."

I did not take her baiting. I walked into the foyer and out of the house. I could hear my mother screaming upstairs and feel my great-aunt's cold eyes burning at my back. I kept walking. If I had to walk all night, I would.

I would never go back. Not now. Not ever.

Chapter Six—Carrie Jo

I woke myself with a scream of pain. The contraction was so powerful that it took my breath away. I had no doubt I was in labor. I had no time to dwell on what I had dreamed. No time to consider Olivia's threats or Karah's emotions. I reached out and suddenly remembered that Ashland wasn't there. He had left early this morning to secure the Happy Go Lucky. Against all odds, Tropical Storm Jasmine was growing and heading our way. Catching my breath, I reached for my cell phone as I tried to sit up. Sweat beaded on my forehead, and I gasped for air. Thankfully the pain eased and the muscles relaxed. I looked at my alarm clock, remembering somehow that I needed to time these contractions.

"You can't come now, baby. You have a few more weeks before you make your appearance. Stay inside where it's safe." My child did not respond as he usually did. He lay quiet and still. And that bothered me. "Hey! I know you hear me. Let Momma know you're okay." Still nothing. Not a kick. Not a punch. He—or she—was as still as…

No, I'm not going there. The baby is fine. I am fine. Everything is going to be okay. Tears of panic welled up in my eyes. Everything *would* be okay, wouldn't it? Only one way to find out. I was going to the hospital. I dressed as quickly as I could in a voluminous summer dress. As I slid it over my head, the next contraction hit me.

"Agh!" I doubled over and managed to ease myself back on the bed. I looked at the clock. Five minutes. These were really far apart. I was in the early stages of labor. I gasped and focused on breathing. I swore at myself for not taking those Lamaze classes when I had the chance. Ashland wanted to go, but I thought it was dopey. I just wanted to get through it with as much dignity as I could and have a healthy baby. Breathing as calmly as I could—*that's what you're supposed to do, right?*—I waited for the pain to ease. When it finally let up, I slid my feet into my sandals and grabbed my overnight bag and purse. By the time I made it to the bottom of the stairs, nearly five minutes had passed. I sat in the foyer chair and waited for the next contraction. I grasped the corner of the table as the pain hit me again. It seemed stronger this time. Oh God! Should I call an ambulance? It would take me at least ten minutes to get to the hospital. There was no way I could drive. Knowing that Ashland probably wouldn't have a signal out on the water, I called Detra Ann.

"Hey, girl!"

Breathing heavily, I said, "Girl, I need you to take me to the hospital."

"Oh my God! Where are you? Is it the baby?"

"Baby, yes. Home. Please come now." My breathing came quick, and I forgot again how I was supposed to breathe.

"I'm on the way now! Henri! Bring me the keys, babe! It's CJ…" She hung up the phone, and I didn't call her back. I scribbled a note for Doreen and left it on the foyer table where I hoped she would find it. I panted through the pain and waited patiently for Detra Ann to show up. When I heard the car screech into the driveway, I opened the door and stood leaning against the doorframe.

"Oh my God! Help me, Henri." She said slowly and loudly, "It's go-ing to be all right, Carrie Jo!"

The pain eased up a bit, and I growled at her. "I'm not deaf, Detra Ann. I'm having a baby."

She didn't seem to mind my snappiness. "I'm calling Ashland now."

"He's going to tie up the boat. He doesn't have a signal out there."

"I'm try-ing any-way, o-kay?"

"Fine!" I said as I rolled into the front seat. "I told you I'm not deaf!"

"Your seat belt!" She reached for me, and I swatted her hand away.

"Oh my God, Detra Ann. If you put that seat belt on me, I'll kill you." She danced around me and climbed in the back, ignoring my crabbiness like the true friend she was.

Henri put on his flashers and drove us to the hospital in record time. "You're right. No answer."

I didn't respond. I stared at my watch and waited for the contraction. I could feel it building, and I knew it would be a strong one. I suddenly prayed I didn't pee on myself. I had to go, and I didn't want to pee in Henri's car.

"This sucks so bad!" I yelled as I clutched the dashboard. We pulled into the ER driveway of Springhill Memorial, and Detra Ann bounced out of the car and inside to get a wheelchair.

A nurse chased her, and together the two women managed to get me into the chair. Henri yelled at us, "I'm going to the marina to get Ashland. I'll be back soon."

"Okay, thanks!" I yelled at him like I was crazy.

"Breathe, Carrie Jo, breathe. It's all right. You are going to be all right. Oh my gosh, I'm going to be an aunt."

"This your sister?" the nurse asked as she pushed me through the double doors.

"Yep," I lied. I knew they wouldn't have let her stay with me if I'd said no. She was like a sister to me. That had to count for something.

For the next fifteen minutes a swarm of nurses worked around me, hooking me up to intimidating machines that supposedly monitored the contractions and my heart rate. The on-call doctor was coming to check my dilation. When she arrived, I cried, "It's too soon. The baby isn't supposed to be here yet. And he's not moving. What's wrong?"

"It's okay. Babies sometimes get still before they are born. If he's in the birth canal, there isn't much room for him to move around. Let's just check." The doctor moved her stethoscope over my stomach and listened intently. As she moved the cold round piece over my stomach, my panic grew. Shouldn't she have found him by now?

"Ah, there he is. He's fine. You want to hear him?" I nodded and accepted the stethoscope. Yes, I could hear his heart beating strong and evenly. I knew he was a boy. I had known it all along. I didn't know why I'd tried to deny it. I tried not to think about what that might mean.

"Let's take a look now. See how far you have to go."

Detra Ann stood at the head of the bed holding my purse and my hand. I looked at her, and she smiled down at me like a cheerleader-angel.

"Hmm…not that far along after all. Only dilated two centimeters."

"That's bad, isn't it? Is the baby going to be okay?"

The doctor smiled patiently. "Yes, he is fine. Early labor happens to many women. Your doctor is on the way. We'll consult, but if the due date is three weeks away, then he'll probably want to stop those contractions for a while." She looked at her watch and said, "If your doctor isn't here within the next half hour, I'll write the order myself. Either way, you'll have to stay overnight so we can keep an eye on you and the baby. We don't need the baby to come today. He needs to wait a bit longer, if possible. Would you like something to help with the pain?"

"No, I think I'm okay for now. I'll wait."

"Okay. I'll be back soon. Hopefully with the orders for that drip. It will stop the contractions. Let the nurse know if you need anything."

She smiled at me and rearranged my blanket before leaving us alone.

Detra Ann put our bags on the nearby table and sat beside me. "Don't worry, CJ. It's going to be fine. You heard the doctor. This happens sometimes. I have seen it in my own family. My cousin Lanie came to the hospital four times before she actually had the baby. She just about wore us out."

"I don't mean to be an inconvenience to anyone."

"That's not what I meant. I hope you know that."

"I'm sorry to be such a jerk. I want the baby to stay where he is because I know he'll be safe in there. What happens when he comes out? What about this curse? I can't stop thinking about it."

"Well, you need to. That baby needs you to think happy thoughts. All right? I mean, think about this in the light of day. Are curses even real? What if it's all just a big coincidence and you're worried over nothing? Lots of people die young. It's not a reason to believe in curses. I think you should tell Ashland and let him worry about it."

"But you were the one who said we shouldn't tell him," I said, frowning at her as I prepared for the next contraction.

"Well, I know, but I changed my mind. If it's going to make you go into labor and make you sick, then you need to tell him."

"Carrie Jo?" I heard a voice call from the doorway.

"Yes?" I answered and froze. It was my mother. "Momma?"

"Yes, it's me. Your housekeeper told me where to find you. I hope it's okay that I came."

It wasn't, but I didn't want to argue with her. I was so shocked at seeing her that I didn't bother to introduce her. She wore a neat dress that came past her knees. To my surprise, it didn't have long sleeves and it wasn't black. It was cobalt blue and completely out of style; she probably bought it at one of her favorite secondhand stores. The dress had a conservative neckline and three-quarter sleeves. She wore cheap shoes and carried an even cheaper black purse. Deidre Jardine had once been a pretty woman; today she wore light pink lipstick and a bit of mascara, which made her look prettier than usual. How long had it been since I had seen her wear makeup? I thought it was against her religion. She had gotten ultra-religious about seven years ago and given up worldly things like makeup and jewelry. I was surprised to see she wore gold stud earrings, like the kind girls wore when they first got their ears pierced.

Before I could say anything else, a wave of pain hit me. I closed my eyes and focused on making it through the agonizing half minute. The machine beside me sputtered out paper and beeped. A nurse appeared and studied the paper. "That's a good one. If you decide you need pain medicine, just yell."

"Breathe, baby," my mother coached me patiently.

"Mom is here too? That's great. Between your sister and your mother, you will do just fine." Thankfully Deidre didn't make a fuss, but when I opened my eyes I could see her looking at Detra Ann questioningly. My friend shrugged and didn't say anything.

"What are you doing here, Momma?"

"Didn't you get my letter, Carrie Jo?"

"Yes, but I haven't had a chance to read it yet. I've been a bit busy."

"I see," she said sadly. "It's not important. What can I do for you?"

"You can tell me why you're here, Deidre." I said curtly. Detra Ann's eyes widened, but she kept her mouth shut.

"I wanted...I didn't know you were having a baby. Your housekeeper told me you were going to the hospital. I didn't mean to interfere. I'll go now." She sounded on the verge of tears. She picked up her purse and headed out the door.

As she disappeared, Detra Ann scowled at me. "I had no idea you could be so mean, CJ. I know y'all are estranged, but she is that baby's grandmother."

"You don't understand," I said woodenly, offering no further explanation.

"You're right, I don't. I'll be right back." She stomped out of the room after my mother and left me alone. I instantly felt guilty. Of course she was right, but she didn't know what I'd been through with Deidre. The humiliating childhood. The horrible teenage years when I couldn't keep friends. Coming home from school to find a circle of strangers praying over your bedroom, touching your things, rebuking the devil. She had done that. Not me. If Detra Ann wanted to be mad at me, so be it.

I lay in the bed, tears sliding down my face, when another contraction came. My phone rang in my purse, but I couldn't reach it. Feeling desperation rise within me, I said a prayer. "It's me, God. I know we don't talk as much as we should, and that's totally my fault, but I need your help. Please protect Ashland and our baby. Help me know what to do because I haven't got a clue."

Just then, Detra Ann came back in. My phone rang again, and she dug it out for me. Without waiting for permission she answered. "Hey, Ash. Sure, she's right here. Everything is fine."

She handed me the phone, and I took it with shaking hands. The contraction was passing, and I felt like myself again. "Hey, babe."

"You okay? I'll be on the way soon. Henri found me."

"Sorry to mess up your day."

"Stop that. You just hold on, okay. I promise you it's going to be all right. You just do what the doctor says and listen to Detra Ann. We'll be together soon, the three of us."

"All right." The tears sprang up again, against my wishes.

"Hey, hey," he said in a low and comforting voice, "don't cry. You can do this. I promise you I'll be there soon."

"I can do this," I repeated obediently. "Be careful."

"Will do. Talk to you soon. Let me speak to Detra Ann."

"All right." I handed the phone back to her. A nurse hustled in the room and reviewed the paper. She let me know my doctor was coming down the hall now. Detra Ann smoothed my hair and kissed my forehead after she hung up the phone.

"That's from Ashland. And me. You know I love you, CJ."

"I love you too." I leaned forward and fell into her arms. We hugged until the next contraction came.

"Is she still here?" We both knew who I meant.

"Yep. She's in the waiting room, crocheting and praying."

"That's good. For once in my life, I'm glad to hear that. I can use all the prayers I can get."

Chapter Seven—Ashland

Everything went wrong that morning. I fell off the boat for the first time ever. The engine didn't want to start, and when I finally thought I would be able to get her going, Henri came running down the pier. I knew right away it was about CJ, and that made the weight of the day feel even heavier.

"Baby is coming, Ashland. She's at the hospital."

"He's not supposed to be here yet." I couldn't help but worry. This wasn't normal, was it?

"Somebody better tell that to the baby because he's absolutely determined to arrive. You want to ride with me?"

"No, I better take mine."

"You sure?" he asked, studying my face.

"No, I'm not sure."

"Get in. I'm driving. You look like you need a minute to think."

"Yeah, probably so." I left the boat where she was, climbed into his Dodge Charger and put on my seat belt. We didn't say much as we drove out of the marina parking lot, but I was glad for his company. I sensed he wanted to say something, but he didn't. I wasn't one to push someone to talk. It was a trait that drove my wife batty.

The dark clouds gathered above us and seemed to increase as we drove. "I can't remember when I saw the sun last. Weather seems weird lately."

"Yeah. You can't ever tell about the weather down here."

"What's going on, Henri? Is it the baby? I can tell there's something you aren't telling me. Don't hold back now. I want to know what's happening. Is Carrie Jo sick or something?"

"As far as I know, the baby is fine. Carrie Jo is fine too. I swear." He was trying to play it cool, but I knew he was holding back. I started to ask him again, but something caught my eye. It was a lone figure standing at the edge of the road. For a millisecond I thought he was alive, but as we approached him I saw that I was wrong. He was a ghost, and if he didn't move, we would drive right through him. His black suit was covered with dust, and it looked like something from the early 1900s. His hair had a dingy white tinge, but his skin was even whiter. Then he jumped into the road as we drove through him, and instinctively I gasped and tried to move out of the way like a wild man. His face lingered in front of mine for a long, agonizing moment, and he grinned at me. His dry, dead lips pulled back from his yellowed teeth. I screamed as he passed through my body, and Henri screamed too. The soul-sucking phantom pulled all the warmth out of me.

Henri slammed on the brakes. "What the hell was that about?" he demanded. "You seeing things?"

"Hell yes!" I said, trying to calm my breathing. I wiped my face furiously with my hands as if I could wipe away the ghostly residue from my soul. "I guess you didn't?"

"No, but I felt something. Coldness. Gone now. It is gone, right?" He glanced over his shoulder into the backseat, and I followed his lead. Nothing there. Thank God.

"Yes, it's gone."

"Anyone we know?"

"Nobody I have ever seen. And I hope I never see him again." I kept my eyes glued to the road ahead and tried not to look around me. So that's why I had been out of sorts this morning. The spirits were back. "I don't think I'll ever get used to this. I thought by talking about it and, you know, embracing it and all that jazz, it would get better. But it hasn't."

"What do you mean?"

I didn't have time for this right now. I had to get to my wife. Why did I even bring it up?

Henri glanced at me and said, "What's up?"

"It's been months since it happened last, so I thought it went away. I've seen things at a distance, but that just now was right in my face. It's like he was taunting me. Laughing at me. Something isn't right."

Henri's jaw clenched, and I could see him struggling with something. We were just ten minutes from the hospital now. "For the love of God, tell me what you know, Henri."

"The girls didn't want to tell you, but there is a rumor...no, that's not it. There is some concern that you might be cursed."

"What?" I said, laughing.

"Carrie Jo wanted to surprise you with a family tree print. You know the swanky kind you hang in a picture frame? During the research, Rachel noticed something strange about the date of expiration for some of your relatives."

"Date of expiration? Rachel is involved with this?"

"I don't know what else you would call it."

"Sorry, go on. You were saying?"

"The bottom line is the men in your family never live past forty. CJ wants to make sure that doesn't happen to you or your son."

"My son," I said, enjoying hearing that. Carrie Jo had been so insistent that we would have a girl. I always knew that was wrong. Even Lenore knew. I wished she were here now to tell me if I was going crazy or not. "Cursed? How can a whole family be cursed? Is that even a legit concern, or is my wife finding things to worry about?"

"I saw the genealogy, and she's not exaggerating. It is a real phenomenon. Your family never talked about this?"

"Not to me. My dad died when I was a kid, and my Uncle Robert...damn. He died too. Both before they were forty. Great. Does that mean at age forty I'm going to keel over?"

Henri said nothing but kept his eyes on the road. Finally, he said, "Stop holding out. Tell me the truth."

"Most of them died right after they turned thirty. Very few made it to forty."

The car hit a pothole and made a crunching noise. It seemed appropriate. Here we were talking about curses, and Henri's car was tearing up.

"So what's the cure?" I asked. "I mean, how do I get rid of this bad mojo or whatever it is? I can't deny I've been in a kind of funk lately, but I chalked it up to being a new dad. Sometimes crap just happens, and up until now it seemed I had no problem with luck. Now I guess that's all changed?"

"It has to have something to do with your gift. Curses are supernatural, and you have a supernatural ability. Where did you get your gift from? Do you know where it started? Did your mother see ghosts? Your father? Anyone give you clues about where this supernatural stuff came from? Maybe if we knew the answers we could trace the curse."

"Not really. My mother talked to the air all the time, but I didn't chalk it up to ghosts. I thought she was just pretending, playacting. I was a kid, so that kind of stuff didn't bother me. Later, though, she really pursued the supernatural, always dragging me to séances and whatnot. I couldn't tell you about my father. He didn't really share things with me."

"Too bad we can't ask your mother."

"Yeah, I know she'd love being a grandmother. She loved children."

There was an awkward silence as we zipped through a yellow light on Government Street. "We could ask her. If you'd be willing."

I bit my fingernail. I had my elbow on the window ledge. It made me feel ready to act if I needed to. Why did I think I could run from a ghost? Hopefully we wouldn't drive through any more of those.

"What are you talking about?"

"A séance would do the trick. I'm sure we could contact her."

I ran my hands through my hair. "I can't even begin to tell you how opposed I am to that idea."

"I figured you would be. CJ mentioned it, but considering what you're up against…. I'm only trying to help."

"I know it, but there has to be another way."

"You're probably right." Henri banked the vehicle to the right. We were close now, just a mile away. I was so anxious to get there I unbuckled my seat belt in anticipation.

"You'll be a great father."

I couldn't help but smile. "You think so?"

"I know so. Here we are. I'll drop you and then follow you up. Don't wait for me."

"Don't worry, I won't," I said with a smile as I practically jumped out of the car. As soon as the smoky glass door slid open, I knew I was in trouble. There in the lobby were two ghosts, and both of them knew I could see them. "Oh great," I muttered to myself.

"Can I help you?" an older lady with a nametag that read 'Dot' asked me. She must have thought I was talking to her.

"No, ma'am. I know where I'm going." I didn't tell her that an old man and a young boy were standing behind her. Why creep her out like that? The two ghosts weren't frightening like the roadside apparition had been. They whispered to one another, and the younger one pointed to me. The boy's hand passed by Dot's ear as he nudged the man. Dot patted her hair-sprayed hair as if she could feel it. Without much more notice to me or her hair, she answered the phone in a bright, cheerful voice, "Springhill Memorial Hospital. How may I direct your call?"

I sailed past her and caught the elevator. The baby floor, as it was affectionately known around here, was the fifth floor. I stood in the elevator with four other people and a ghost. He had a slack jaw, and the remnants of yellow hair circled his large head. Suddenly as if a magnet drew him, he moved closer to me. He stared at me with his empty gray eyes. "You know, don't you? You know where she is. Tell me," he pleaded with me. I tried not to fly across the elevator and scare the other passengers. As soon as the door opened I jumped ahead of the ladies who stood closest to it. "Tell me!" the ghoul screamed after me. I had gotten off on the wrong floor. Two more levels to go now. I flew past a crowd of people; I wasn't sure if they were dead or alive, and thankfully none of them followed me into the stairwell. By the time I made it to the fifth floor, I was so panicked I had to stop and catch my breath. I heard a sound behind me. Peering down the railing above me was another specter, a ghostly janitor with bloodless skin. His phantom mop plunked to the ground, and he eased down the steps toward me.

"Oh God, oh Jesus!" I prayed loudly. To my relief the words seemed to repel him enough to give me time to slip out the door. I pushed open the door from the stairwell and stepped onto the fifth floor. The atmosphere was very different here. Instead of lingering spirits and angry black clouds, there was an abundance of light and a thick, peaceful feeling. I breathed a sigh of relief as I walked to the nurses' station.

A young nurse with a dazzling white smile greeted me. I said, "I'm here to see my wife, Carrie Jo Stuart."

"Yes, Mr. Stuart. Follow me." She stood to show me the way. She wore yellow scrubs with tiny rainbows all over them. Very cheerful.

"No need to bother yourself. Just point me in the right direction."

She smiled and waved to the left. "She's that way. Room 542."

I glanced down the hall, making sure I had the right direction, and then turned back to her to say thanks. "Thank you…" The nurse was gone. She'd vanished in just a second.

Another woman walked up. "May I help you?"

"No, I know the way."

All I could think of was getting to my wife and son. I needed this day to be over soon. I couldn't take much more. The window at the end of the hallway suddenly clouded. The sunshine departed. Storm clouds were rolling in.

Somehow, it seemed appropriate.

Chapter Eight—Ashland

Detra Ann hugged me and, as she typically did, fussed over me and brought me endless cups of coffee. Carrie Jo looked beautiful, but I didn't bother telling her so. She wouldn't believe me, and it didn't seem like the most sensitive thing to say during this painful and stressful process. Thankfully her doctor finally ordered the medicine that would stop the contractions. Carrie Jo had been in pain for several hours. She didn't complain, but I hated seeing the woman I loved suffer. The drip took effect quickly, and her contractions weakened. I breathed a sigh of relief knowing that Baby Boy would be indoors a little longer.

Baby Boy. Funny name, but I liked it. If my wife and I couldn't settle on a mutually approved baby name, I'd be forced to call him that. Now that his arrival was closer, I wondered how important names were anyway. I kissed CJ's hand and didn't say too much. I let the nurses do their work and tried to keep out of the way. I kept my eyes trained on my wife and not the creatures that occasionally sailed past the door or popped in to stare at me.

Seeing ghosts wasn't like the movies. Not at all. The spirits weren't trying to communicate with me or convince me to help them. Not in any kind of coherent way. Most of the ghosts I saw were a little eccentric—a bit mad, really. It was more like they sensed I was different, and that difference drove them even crazier. I got the sense that when you died, if you didn't pass on to wherever you were supposed to, you were left to amble about the spirit world trapped in your own nightmare. It wasn't a fate I wished on anyone. Especially someone I loved.

I used to believe that like Carrie Jo, I would get better at my "gift" or whatever you wanted to call it. But it hadn't happened for me, no matter how many books I read or how much I practiced. The appearance of a ghost scared the hell out of me every single time. Regardless of how much I prepared to see one, they always caught me by surprise. I prayed constantly, more so than I ever had before, but so far my prayers appeared to be unanswered. At least I had my friends, and until this latest session of ghost-seeing passed, I would keep them close. The more living beings around me the better.

Here we were all crowded in the room together now. The living collective appeared to repel the majority of the ghosts. Of the six of us, CJ and me plus Rachel, Chip, Detra Ann and Henri, only Henri and I knew what was happening. He looked at me encouragingly but like a true friend kept his mouth shut. One nurse complained about the number of people visiting, but I assured her it was okay. I was pretty sure I hadn't heard the end of her unhappiness, but let her try and run them out.

Suddenly everyone got quiet again. The machine bleeped to life as Carrie Jo squeezed my hand and sweated through another contraction. "I'm good, babe. Promise. I'm good," she whispered as she turned in the bed trying to find a comfortable spot. Miss Henrietta, the name I gave the unhappy nurse, came back in a deeper frown on her face.

"Okay, everyone. I have to insist you step out. The doctor is coming to check Mrs. Stuart again. If she hasn't dilated any more, he'll probably send her home. Clear the room," she said with a wave of her hand.

CJ frowned at her. "It's not like I haven't been trying," she sassed back at her. "Go ahead, babe. I'll be fine."

I kissed her forehead and walked out with a growing feeling of dread. Henri stayed close. "I've got your six, Ashland," he whispered as we stepped outside.

"Detra Ann, is she going to be okay? What's going on?" A petite brunette stood between us and the waiting room. Her dress hung off her small shoulders, and her lips quivered nervously.

"Oh yes, she's fine, Mrs. Jardine. I don't believe you have met Carrie Jo's husband yet. This is Ashland Stuart."

If she'd told me the woman was the pope, I wouldn't have been more surprised. I extended my hand to her and studied her face. Now that I knew she was CJ's mother, I could see the resemblance. "I didn't know you were here. I'm sorry. I would have come to speak to you sooner had I known."

"I'm sure it's not something my daughter would want everyone to know. We haven't been on the best terms, but I do care about her," she offered as a kind of apology. Her bright hazel eyes glossed with tears, but I was suspicious. I knew what Carrie Jo had been through with this woman. The nervous lady before me hardly appeared threatening, but looks were almost always deceiving.

"Her doctor is with her right now. Maybe when he completes his exam you can see her. If she's up to it," I said carefully.

"I saw her earlier, but only for a few minutes. I'll see her when she's ready. As long as she's okay. I had no idea she was having a baby."

As she spoke, a young spirit sailed past, holding a bundle of blankets in her arms. I tried not to stare at the ghost, but she stared at me, her pale face too close to mine. Mrs. Jardine turned around to investigate. I couldn't be sure, but as she faced me again I thought I saw her eyes widen a bit. Could she see the girl too? The spirit paused to listen to our conversation, but when no one acknowledged her she began to fade away. That was something else I had learned about the spirit world. The more attention you gave the creatures, the stronger they became. In some cases simply ignoring them was enough to send them back to wherever they came from.

I shivered involuntarily, and Henri touched my shoulder. "You need anything?" he asked.

"Coffee?" Detra Ann offered me.

"Please, no more coffee. I'll be up for the next two days if I drink another cup," I said as she frowned at me.

"Mr. Stuart, the doctor would like to talk to you." The crotchety nurse waved me back to CJ's room, and I excused myself from the gathering. Chip and Rachel crowded around Mrs. Jardine and asked her about her stay in Mobile. I was glad to see it. I didn't have a bad feeling about her, regardless of her history with Carrie Jo.

"Mr. Stuart, nice to see you."

"Dr. Gary. Good to see you too. Are we having a baby tonight?"

"I was just telling your wife that she's made some progress. She's dilated to four centimeters now, but I'd like to wait if the baby will allow it. She isn't due for a few more weeks, and that time is crucial for good lung development. I know you're miserable, dear," the older man said to Carrie Jo as he squeezed her hand, "but if you two can hold out a little longer, it will be better for both of you." He turned to me and continued, "Mrs. Stuart appears to be responding well to the medications; the contractions have diminished, and that's a good sign. I'd like to keep her overnight, just to watch her. If all goes well, I'll send her home in the morning, and then we'll see what Junior decides to do." Relieved, I hugged the doctor. He good-naturedly patted my back. "I know it's a nerve-racking process for both of you, but I assure you that you will get through it and everyone will be fine. The baby's heartbeat is strong and steady. Mother's health is good too. I see nothing to worry about."

"Thanks, doc. That is good news."

"I'll see you two in the morning."

"Thank you, Dr. Gary," CJ called as he walked out the door. "Sorry, babe. Didn't mean to make you worry about me," she said with a small smile.

I kissed her forehead again and sat in the chair beside her. "You had nothing to do with it. You heard the doctor. It's up to Baby Boy, not you."

She wrinkled her nose at me. "That's the name you want?"

"Well, no. It's just a nickname I came up with."

"You're convinced he'll be a he, aren't you?"

I couldn't help but grin. This moment was the happiest I had been all day. I nodded and confessed, "From day one."

"All right, so what names do you have in mind?"

"Really?"

"Yep, whatcha got?"

I squeezed her hand and said, "I was thinking Richard or James."

"Aren't those Bible names?"

I laughed aloud. "I don't think there were any Richards in the Bible."

She laughed too and wiped tears from her eyes. "We're going to be okay, right? No matter what?"

"No matter what. Yes, we will be fine."

I held her until we heard a knock on the door. It was Carrie Jo's mother. "Hi. I just wanted to say goodbye before I go back to the hotel. It's getting dark, and I don't really know my way around here. I'll be praying for you, Carrie Jo."

CJ looked at me, and I smiled at her as if to say, *It's okay. I'm right here.*

"Stay for a minute, Momma." That delighted the older woman to no end, and she dropped her purse in the chair and walked to the bedside. As she and CJ talked, Henri and Detra Ann stepped in the room to watch us. Detra Ann waved me over, and we walked outside for a minute.

"Listen, I know they have a rough history, but her mother is telling the truth. She didn't know CJ was pregnant, and she really does care about what happens to her. Let Carrie Jo know, okay?"

"Yeah, I will."

"Henri told you, didn't he?"

"I knew anyway. I just didn't know what to call it."

"So you think you're cursed?"

"Who's cursed?" Mrs. Jardine asked, standing a few feet away.

Detra Ann piped up, "It's just a figure of speech. Ashland's had some bad luck lately is all."

Without waiting for an invitation, Carrie Jo's mother grabbed my hand and began to pray, "Dear God, break this curse on this young man's life. No weapon formed against him will prosper, just as your Word says. Keep him safe as he fights the good fight. Amen."

Surprised by the impromptu prayer, I murmured "Amen" and thanked her.

"No need to thank me. I can't have my only son-in-law cursed. I'll keep praying. That's something I know how to do." She smiled brightly, and I had to admit, I did feel better. My space wasn't ghost-free, but the spirits had diminished a bit and none were in my face. Always a plus. "Your friend said he'd take me home. I'll come back in the morning, if that's okay."

"Sure. Carrie Jo is supposed to go home in the morning, but I'm not sure what time. Are you sure you're comfortable at the hotel? Which one are you staying at?"

"Don't worry about me. I am very comfortable in my room. You be with your wife."

"Hey!" Detra Ann said. "I'll ride too. Here comes Henri now. See you in the morning, Ash." She kissed my cheek, and I could feel her glossy lipstick on my skin. I waved goodbye and hurried back to CJ's room.

She'd snuggled up in the blankets and had her eyes closed. She stirred and made sure I was there, then went back to sleep. A few hours later I hunkered down in the chair and thought about the simple prayer that Deidre had said over me. It comforted me, and soon I fell asleep.

Chapter Nine—Carrie Jo

Before nine o'clock, Ashland and I were headed home. I'd made it through the night with no other contractions, and we both breathed a sigh of relief. I think everyone thought I would be disappointed that the baby's arrival had been delayed, but I wasn't. Not at all. As long as Baby Boy stayed close to me, I knew I could protect him. *Oh no! Did I just call him Baby Boy?* I smiled at Ashland and shook my head.

"What?" he asked innocently.

"You. You've got me calling our son Baby Boy."

"You're okay with a son, then?"

I leaned back against the seat and smiled even bigger. "Yep, I'm okay with it. I don't know why I was so dead set against having a boy." We pulled into the driveway and weren't a bit surprised to see cars already there. Doreen's old truck was on the street, and of course Rachel's and Detra Ann's vehicles were in the driveway.

"I know why. And I know what you think."

Suddenly all the brightness of the day seemed to vanish. One of my well-meaning friends must have told Ashland what we discovered, and now he was going to say it—the word I didn't dare say.

"I know about the curse, Carrie Jo."

There. He said it. Now it was real.

For all three of us.

I couldn't meet his eyes, so I stared at the yard. It was so sad-looking, with dead flowers and moldy sidewalks. How did they get moldy? We had the place power-washed just two months ago. It sure as heck didn't look like it.

"Now what, babe? How do we break it?"

"*We* can't break it, Carrie Jo, but you can help *me* figure it out. This is my deal. And I want you to promise me something."

"What's that?" I asked suspiciously.

"I don't want you to do anything that will put you or our son in danger. Our son…yeah, I like that." He squeezed my hand. "I couldn't stand it if I knew you two were in danger. I mean it, CJ. Nothing. No visiting the house. No stirring up spirits. You let me do this. Okay?"

I bit my lip and searched his face for any kind of softness. There was none to be found. He was dead serious about this. "If you won't promise for me, do it for Baby Boy."

My hands rubbed my stomach as our son adjusted his foot, shoving it deeper into my ribs as if to say, "Yeah, I agree with Dad."

"Okay, I promise not to do any of those things."

It was his turn to be suspicious. "And don't do anything else I haven't thought of yet, okay?"

"Scout's honor." I held up two fingers. "Now let's go in the house before the bottom falls out. It looks pitch black out here. The weather is so unpredictable."

"This has got to be from Hurricane Jasmine—the storm is on the way, but it's only a Cat 1. We'll be okay." He chuckled at Rachel waving from the front door. "Looks like we're home base this time around. I guess that's fair since we camped out with Henri for the last tropical storm. Do I need to send everyone home?"

"No, I like having our friends around. This storm will be like the last one, I'm sure. It will fizzle out before it gets here."

"Looks like we have an extra guest."

I could see my mother's petite figure through the big bay window. How did I miss her? I sighed and nodded. Ash didn't need me losing it right now, and so far Momma had behaved. I promised myself I would get to the bottom of her appearance here right away, though. I couldn't have my baby around someone so judgmental, so unpredictable.

Stop being so negative, Carrie Jo. What if she's changed?

I had given her chances before. I loved her, no doubt about it, but it was easier not dealing with her. Not talking to her. Not hoping things would change. Yeah, that was way easier than seeing her, daydreaming about a "normal" relationship. Here we were, dealing with a curse, and she showed up out of the blue. What was up with that? She did seem different, but maybe that was also a ploy. The old Deidre Jardine would have recited at least five Bible verses at me by now. I wondered what she was up to. I hoped and prayed this wasn't about money.

Doreen came barreling out the door. "Here she is! Mrs. Stuart! I am so glad to see you. You had me worried! No baby yet, huh? No worries. He will come in his own good time. I stocked your pantry for the storm, but I didn't know all these people would be here. Do I need to make another trip to the store?"

I smiled at her and followed her into the kitchen. "Hey, everyone!" I waved to the rest of the group camped around the widescreen television in the living room. "No, Doreen. This is fine. You didn't even need to do that. If we need something else, I'm sure one of these guys will go. I hope you made me some fruit salad. I'm starving."

"Of course. Right on the top shelf. Just for you."

"You go home and be with Stephan. Are you staying in Mobile?"

"Oh no. I never stay for these storms, and I wish you would go too. We go to Stephan's mother's house in Evergreen. No storms there." I smiled at her and insisted that she go home. The skies were darkening, and according to the local weather reports that blared from the next room, Hurricane Jasmine would be bearing down on us in the next few hours. I didn't know what it was about hurricanes that made my friends want to gather around a television. But I imagined that was the way it would be for the next few days. I was glad. I wanted them close to me right now. And close to Ashland.

"I am sorry about your puppy, Mrs. Stuart. He was a sweet dog."

"Thanks, Doreen. Me too. You go to Stephan now. I'm fine. We'll see you when this is over."

With a nervous wave, she grabbed her purse and left out the kitchen door.

Doreen's powder blue Ford backed out of the driveway, and I waved at her as she pulled into the frantic street. Pretty busy out there. Hm…maybe I did need to pay attention. It was dark enough for the streetlights to come on already. Yep, this was going to be a doozy of a storm.

"Hey, babe. I have to go to the boat. I never did get her secured, and I'd hate to lose her. We've had some happy memories there."

"Ashland…shh…" I said, giggling and kissing him. We had long speculated that we'd conceived during an overnight trip on the Happy Go Lucky.

"Relax. No one can hear me." He kissed me back. "Henri's going with me. Won't be gone but about an hour."

"Sure, but hurry back. No hanging out on the boat."

"In this weather? No way, crazy lady." He laughed and shook his head. "Be back in a bit."

"Better be," I said, kissing him square on the lips before smacking his behind playfully.

"Be kind to your mother," he said to me before he walked out the door. For a second I thought I heard Chunky Boy whine after him as he always did. Chunky Boy and Baby Boy. What a pair they would have made! I sniffled and felt someone beside me.

"You want a cup of tea?" That someone was my mother.

"Yes, but could you make sure it's herbal? Caffeinated drinks make the baby very active."

"Good idea. I was hoping we could talk. Your friends went upstairs to put your shower gifts away. Looks like you were really blessed with all those gifts."

I followed behind her. My back felt sore, but I reasoned it was from the hospital bed. That had been one long night and one stiff mattress. "I have to ask, Momma. Please don't take this the wrong way, but why are you here? I haven't heard from you in over two years. Now you're here?"

She put the lid on the teapot and set it on the stove. "Cut to the chase, hmm? Sometimes you remind me of your Aunt Maggie so much."

"I don't want to talk about Aunt Maggie, Momma. I want to talk about you. And me. It can't be like it used to be. I won't let it be. That's not what I want for my child."

She nodded and looked me square in the eye. She didn't argue or get defensive. "Okay, cards on the table." She sat across from me at the small, round breakfast table. "About a year ago, I had what they called a cardiac event." I waited to hear what else she would tell me. I would hold my sympathy until after I heard the rest of the story. Not that she would lie about such a thing. Deidre Jardine was many things but not a liar. "I am fine now. They put two stents in me, but I can do everything I used to do."

"Sorry to hear that. Does heart disease run in our family?" I wasn't asking for me. What about the baby?

"Not that I am aware of. I know it's a bit of a shock seeing me after so long, but I've come to realize something." Just then the teapot screamed and Deidre got up to pour our cups. I didn't hurry her, but I was dying to hear what she had to say.

Setting the cup in front of me, she stirred in a cube of sugar and put her spoon down. "I don't blame you for not trusting me. For wanting to keep me away. I needed help, Carrie Jo, and I didn't know how to ask for it."

"What kind of help, Momma?"

She laughed nervously. "I'm still not sure. But I have made peace with the Big Man Upstairs. That happened when I thought I was going to die. You know how you hear that your life plays before your eyes when you are dying?" I nodded, unable to sip my tea or even move. I couldn't distract her now, just when she was about to tell me something significant. I could feel it rising, like the crest of a wave. "Well, that's not what happened to me. I didn't see my life—I saw yours."

"Really?"

"Yes. And I had no idea. It was like I could feel what you felt, see what you saw. I realized that while I thought I was protecting you, loving you, saving you, Carrie Jo, I was terrorizing you instead. Every incident. The time I came to the classroom to get you after Ginny's stepfather...I walked through that whole thing as you." When she met my eyes, the hazel color appeared a bit green now. I had forgotten they changed color like that. "You needed someone to protect you from me. I hurt you. In my desire to shield you, I did the thing I dreaded. Please believe me, protecting you was really all I wanted to do."

"Protecting me from what?"

"From who I was. And who I was afraid you'd become."

"I don't know what you mean." The baby moved around, and I rubbed my stomach to still him. "Tell me what you mean."

"Where do you think you got your dream walking from?"

"Dream walking?"

"Yes, that's what my mother used to call it."

"Used to call what?" I asked incredulously.

"Going back in time and sometimes forward, through dreams."

I heard a puppy whine somewhere. Must have been the neighbor's dog. A vehicle with a screaming siren whizzed past my home and down the bumpy street. I held my breath as she whispered the truth at last.

"You, my daughter, come from a long line of dream walkers."

Chapter Ten—Ashland

"Ash, you have to call me back. Like ASAP!" Libby's voicemail sounded urgent, as if someone's life hung in the balance. As Henri navigated the traffic, I dialed her office number. I had enough stress in my life right now without Libby losing her mind on me. She wasn't the one being sued. By multiple people.

Without saying "Hello" or "How's your wife?" she immediately began throwing a tantrum. "It's like I said! Someone opened the floodgates. It's open season on Ashland Stuart. What the hell did you do? Post your net worth on a forum? We have another lineage claim! Myron and Alice Reed, whoever the hell they are! And just to make it worse, plaintiffs Rhodes and Hines have teamed up and are asking for nothing less than half—of everything!"

"Hello to you too, Libby. In case you haven't noticed, we are in the middle of a hurricane right now. Can't this wait? I can't imagine the wheels of justice moving so quickly that I need to head to the courthouse right this minute. That has never been the case."

"Screw the hurricane! Aren't you listening? You are in major trouble, Ashland." She was talking too loud in my ear; I held the phone away from my head and seriously considered throwing it out the window into the gray, choppy waters of the Mobile Bay. I should never have hired Libby. Once again I let my loyalties to friends and family get me into trouble. And my track record with lawyers wasn't the greatest. Henri shook his head in surprise at Libby's tone but kept his eyes on the dangerous roads.

I put the phone back to my ear. "Okay, reality check, Libby. You work for me, remember? Bring your voice down and breathe between sentences. I don't need this right now, so say what you need to say and be done with it. Now what happened?"

"I got a phone call about a half hour ago from a clerk in Judge Carmichael's office."

My phone beeped, and I glanced at it quickly. It was Rachel. Probably wanting me to pick up something for Carrie Jo, like those chicken-flavored crackers she snacked on constantly. I'd have to call her back after I handled this situation. "And?"

"It's true. All of it. Those jerks down at Rodney and Waite came up with this idea—no doubt about it. It's bad, Ash. Whoever drew up your mother's will left a lot of loopholes for crazies to jump through. Unbelievable! The only thing you can do now is settle with these people, and quickly. Then we can make the changes to the original document official and stop the bleeding. I think you need to start thinking of a number you can live with, and let's get them to the table. It's the only way you'll be able to walk away with at least the shirt on your back."

My blood boiled as I listened to the not-so-surprising news. Who in the world sues someone just because they share some DNA? Now the Reeds too? This was unreal. "What? Listen, I'm not prepared to talk about this today."

There was suddenly a deafening silence. "This isn't like you, Ashland. How can you be so blasé about being sued? Don't you understand what I'm saying? Come see me now, and we can get the prelim stuff squared away. I'm sure Carrie Jo would understand. How can I help you if you won't let me?"

"I'll come to your office Monday, after this storm blows through. My wife comes first, Libby. In case you weren't paying attention, we are about to have a baby."

"Well, I *know*," she said with an extra edge of snark to her voice. "I was at your shower, remember? But I would think you'd want to protect your child from all these lawsuits. And I doubt this storm is anything to worry about. It's down to Category 1 status now. Just come by. I've got lunch."

"Goodbye, Libby."

I hung up the phone, shaking my head, turned on the radio and stared at the rising water. We had time to make our trip to the Fairhope Pier and back, but beyond that would be sketchy.

High winds are expected. Hurricane Jasmine has produced gusts up to eighty miles per hour, and she's just getting started. Let's go to Meg, who has an update on this surprisingly powerful storm...

"When it rains, it pours, huh?" Right on cue, fat raindrops slapped the windshield and soon covered the car in sheets of water.

"Literally. If there was any doubt about it before, there isn't now. I've definitely stepped in a streak of bad luck. Are you sure you want to be riding in a car with me?" It was a joke, albeit a bad one, but Henri didn't laugh.

"Stop making that your confession, Ashland. You'll only make a curse stronger by agreeing with it."

"Yeah, whatever." I paid no attention to the spirit that stood in the waters off the causeway. We were driving too fast for him to reach us. At least, I hoped.

"Curses aren't bad luck. Bad luck happens to everyone. That's not the same thing as a curse."

"I'm listening."

"Curses that affect generations of people have to have some weight behind them. You can't just speak a few negative words about someone and hope it hurts them. For a true curse to work and affect a family for generations, there had to have been some major wrong done to someone. Its source must be a great injustice. A wrong that needs to be made right."

"I get that, and I believe it, but how am I supposed to know what that is?"

"Do you believe in God, Ashland?"

We sloshed along the causeway and turned off the bridge onto Highway 98. The watery streets were nearly empty, except for a few people making last-minute provisions. I thought about his question; it was important to answer truthfully. "I've always believed there was, and I still do, but I have a lot of questions for him. If I ever get to see him."

"Do you talk to him at all?"

"Are you asking me if I pray? Sure, I pray." My mood went from bad to worse. This wasn't the time to be having a heart-to-heart about my spiritual life. "What's your point, Henri? Cut to the chase."

"Well, I'm trying to say that I don't have the answers, and even if Lenore was here with us, she wouldn't either. Carrie Jo can't find out, because she's in no shape to perform her 'dream' detective work. Rachel knows about curses but nothing specific about your case. Yet you say you're seeing ghosts again, right?"

"Yep, unfortunately."

"I think God is trying to talk to you, Ashland. I think you have to trust him to show you the truth. If you haven't already, ask him to reveal the source of the curse to you. Tell him you are willing to make right whatever wrong has been done. That's what I would do, if I were in your shoes. Because when you boil it all down, it's about you. This is your battle, and it always has been. From the finding of the Beaumont treasure to the battle in the ballroom. You've been the focus of all this spiritual activity, although it's not always been in an obvious way. God sent you Carrie Jo, and us, if I may say so, but this battle has been for Ashland Stuart."

The car came to a stop at the marina, and we sat in the parking lot. The windshield wipers sloshed back and forth, slinging the water onto the already soaked pavement.

I knew every word he said was true. It had been about me. I'd spent all my time trying to protect Carrie Jo, but Seven Sisters had been *my* house. The Beaumont treasure was also mine. The ghosts had been from *my* past. Now this curse threatened my son and someday my grandsons. Unless I stopped it.

"Pray with me, Henri. I don't know what to say."

He nodded and grabbed my hand. "Lord, nothing is hidden from you, for you see all things—everything in the past, present and future. I know you can see this man's heart and his desire to break this curse over his life and his family. Please, Lord, speak to Ashland. Speak in a language he will understand. Show him what he needs to know. Show him what to do. Give him what he needs to set himself and his family free. We put this in your hands and trust that you will give the answer. In Jesus' name, amen."

"Amen," I whispered. I wiped my eyes and stared at my boat rocking in the marina. I hoped he was right. "Well, no time like the present."

"Need some help?"

"Sure, come on. Let's move her away from the floating dock—that's the worst place to leave a boat during a hurricane. Hey, actually, you should move the car to the other side of the marina. That's where I'm taking the boat. I'll meet you over there."

"All right."

I got out of the car and was soaked to the bone before I'd taken two steps. I walked quickly to the Happy Go Lucky and dug for the keys in my wet pants pocket. I untied the boat and turned the key.

Click, click.

"Come on, are you kidding me?"

I adjusted the throttle and turned the key again.

Click, click.

Smacking the dashboard in frustration, I tapped the gas tank gauge. How the heck was I out of gas? I went below deck and grabbed a half-empty can. It wasn't much, but it would be enough to get me the few yards I needed to travel. The boat rocked and rolled in the rough water of the Mobile Bay. My phone rang in my pocket again, and I suddenly remembered I needed to call Rachel back. I climbed the steps, shielding my eyes from a spray of water with my hand.

I couldn't answer the phone now. Suddenly the wind became so savage I could barely stand up. I waited until the blast of wind passed, then raced to the tank. With clumsy hands I poured the gas into the tank and replaced the gas cap. Closing the outer cap, I stowed the empty can under the railing, latching it secure with a bungee cord. Just as I stood up, the boat lurched, sending me hurtling across the deck.

As I struggled to get up, I thought I saw someone standing near me. It wasn't Henri. It was a woman—it had to be. She wore a moldy dress with a torn hem. I tried to look up to see her face when I felt and heard the sound of wood hitting the side of my head. *Wait!* I thought as the blow came. The boat tilted again, and this time I rolled into the water.

The shattering pain overwhelmed me. I slipped down, down, down...

Chapter Eleven—Olivia

As I waited for my host to join me in the garden, I watched a line of black ants steal sugar crumbs off the top of a forgotten cake. I felt no need to interrupt their work, nor did I feel a great deal of sympathy for the person who would leave such a treat unprotected in a den of ants. I did not accept the mint tea offered me or eat any of the sweet delicacies before me. Isaiah took his time. I knew it was his way of toying with me, reminding me who had the upper hand.

Of all the confrontations I could have hoped to avoid in this life, and I was not one to fear anyone, this would be the one I dreaded the most. I was about to face the man I rejected to marry another. Why did men believe that a woman who possessed a modicum of attractiveness could not possibly be sensible? That a woman must always be guided by the heart or its inclinations?

I was and had always been a sensible woman. I had not come in tears, as I was sure my sister would have done if she had been in my shoes. And I had not come as a servant—I had come as a Beaumont, the last Beaumont, unless God saw fit to give me another child, which seemed unlikely considering my age. In my world, women who were twenty and five and had not had a child were considered old maids, barren, cast-off spinsters. They were whispered about and never invited to social events. Useless dried husks without value.

I had a child, a girl-child, whom I had summarily given up to have the marriage alliance I preferred. I lied to her and told her that she belonged to my brother; it was better for her to believe that. Better for everyone. But Isaiah would not likely be willing to ignore the truth. Our daughter, Isla, had seduced her own uncle Jeremiah, and from that unholy union had come Karah. No, I doubted that Isaiah would be pleased at all.

And I knew he would never let me forget my change of heart, especially now. Not when he heard the whole truth. But still I was here, despite my better judgment, and I had a purpose.

Isaiah must make this right.

The fool girl, our own daughter, convinced her uncle to sign a codicil that named only her children as his heirs. If she'd just left things alone! Claudette and I had arranged a settlement for Christine's youngest daughter, Delilah, and God knew where poor Calpurnia was, probably at the bottom of the Mobile River. My personal investigation into the matter had revealed nothing. It was as if the girl had disappeared from the face of the Earth. Everything had been perfectly arranged until Isla and her schemes interfered. Since there was no male heir between her and Jeremiah, and Karah's parentage was being questioned by the courts—also thanks to Isla—the Cottonwood property, including the missing Beaumont fortune, would go to Jeremiah's brother, Isaiah.

All of it. The irony of the situation did not escape me. He would have what he had lost. But he would never have me.

I had not seen my former lover in ages. For the first five years, he would send me the occasional vague letter asking again why I had rejected him. I never responded.

In the first pleading correspondences, he shared the depth of his despair and pledged his undying love. "I shall never feel again what I felt with you, my darling. Oh, have mercy on me and let me hear you call me that once more. I could have any wife I choose, but my only desire is for you, my own Olivia."

I would admit this to no one, but I kept those letters. On the many nights when I was alone, I would unfold them and read them again and again, pretending that I would write him back. How could I explain to him why I did what I did? I could not, so I never picked up a pen.

Lost in my silent reverie, I did not hear the dogs barking at first, but then I saw Isaiah approaching. He leaned on a silver-headed cane and wore a finely woven black suit that had obviously been made for his trim body. He wore no hat, and I could see that time had been kind to him. He had all his beautiful dark hair, now flecked with white. I did not ask why he used the cane. I still had my manners when I wanted them.

Without a word, he sat down across the small table from me. Spotting the ants, he snapped his fingers and the dogs came running. He put the china dish on the ground, and the nearest hound devoured the food. Isaiah did not seem to care that his dog's pawing and excited eating broke the fine dish.

I raised an eyebrow but said nothing. With some swagger he leaned back in his chair and stared at me. I could see he was taking in every line, every change, every less than firm inch of my skin. He did not hide his amusement at my appearance or my situation. He had the advantage, and he enjoyed it.

This was not going to be easy, I feared. It was he who spoke first.

"This business with the codicil. Did you plan this, Olivia? Was that your plan all along? To use our daughter to seduce her uncle?"

"What kind of woman do you think I am, Isaiah?"

He spun his walking stick and said, "The kind of woman who leaves her intended at the altar while she runs off to marry another. The kind of woman who refuses to tell me where my child is or what's become of her. That's the kind of woman you are, dear Olivia."

"You can't think that I…"

"Can't I?" He smiled at me, rubbing the silver horse head atop his cane.

"To what end? I am not clever enough to dream up such a scenario. I can only assume it was Fate that caused these things to happen."

"Ah." His eyes looked playful. "As do I. It was Fate that left me the inheritance, all the inheritance, Olivia. See, you should have married me, for it was always mine anyway. And I would have loved you without it. That is the truth. Now I will have the fortune without your love. Things change, my dear, and so have I. I found peace with my wife, Virginia, and she has given me many sons and even a daughter. So you see, it was the Hand of Providence that led you away from me to marry Calloway James Torrence, that well-known adulterer. How is life with the old man now? Is he even still alive? My wife tells me you have no children. Well, besides our child."

"You have no right to speak so personally to me! I am not a child anymore, Isaiah." I stood, ready to leave immediately. "You have not changed at all. You are a small man, ruled by your pride and ambition, and obviously I cannot reason with you. Do the right thing, Isaiah. You must set this codicil aside and leave Christine and Jeremiah's original will to stand."

"Too hasty, my dear. You always end things too hastily. I am sure you want to hear me out on this. I have something to say to you, Olivia. Or rather, I have someone you should see."

He rang a little silver bell on the table, and to my utter surprise our daughter walked down the leaf-covered path to our outdoor dining space. She mocked me with a curtsy and sat next to Isaiah in an outfit that was obviously intended for the stage. She showed far too much cleavage, and I kept my face a mask as she leaned forward and kissed her father on the mouth like a wanton.

"Isla, I told you to stay home! What are you doing here?"

"Imagine my surprise, Aunt Olivia, to learn that this man, Isaiah Cottonwood, is my own father. Imagine my great surprise! For I am *truly* surprised! And an even greater surprise, *Aunt* Olivia, is that you are my *mother*! Can you imagine how surprised I was to learn this? You tricked me, Mother! What can that mean for my daughter, Karah? That her father was also her great-uncle? We are one big happy family now, aren't we?" Isla walked toward me with a rare, serious look on her face. "And I want what belongs to me. I will not let this go. You should know that by now."

She got in my face and smiled. "You left me with the general, and he took his liberties with me, Mother. His hands were all over my body. When he got bored with violating and hurting me himself, he invited his friends to do the same. I learned many tricks from the general. Cruel to the last was he, but in the end, I took care of him. One last time. And there were others too, all except my sweet Captain. And even he failed me like all the rest. But now I have my own father!" She walked over to stand beside him, her hand on his shoulder. "He will make sure I get what I deserve. Won't you, Father?"

She slapped the table and yelled at me, "I told you that you would never take Seven Sisters away from me! That it was mine. That it belonged to me. Now we know why, don't we? I will live there until the day I die. Then my daughter…"

"No, you are coming home with me. I have left you too long in this world." I masked my shock, regret and revulsion. I would deal with those later.

"You cannot command me, Mother," she said in a mocking voice.

"Maybe not, but I have legal custody of you until your next court appearance. You *will* go where I command you."

"She can't, can she, Father?" Her sickeningly sweet voice was too much to bear. I left the two of them at the table, her giggles in my ears. Isaiah did not call after me, nor did I wish him to. I left his estate at Park Hill and headed back to Seven Sisters. This was too heartbreaking. I decided I would retrieve my ill-begotten daughter tomorrow and go home. That would be that. I would tell my husband the truth about our fortune and let him do what he could to solve the problem. He might even abandon me, as would be his right. I had failed to deliver a fortune or a child. I was doubly cursed.

As I finished dinner alone, Stokes came in. I could tell by the way the old man shuffled his feet that he wanted to announce someone. "Who is it, Stokes?"

"It's Isaiah Cottonwood."

"I see. Well, let him in, please."

Twice in one day. Apparently, Isaiah had thought of something else to hurt me with. What would he do now, bring Karah before me?

"I am sorry to call on you so late. I realize this is most inopportune of me."

I did not rise. I wiped my hands on a thick linen napkin and waited for him to get to the matter at hand. "Why have you come, Isaiah?"

"I come because—I wanted to tell you—she's not…"

"Ah, Isla," I said, smiling at him sadly.

"I do not know how it happened, but it did happen. I was asleep, and the next thing I remember was her naked body on top of mine. I hardly know how to say this to a lady, but when I woke up, we were… she was…." He shuddered, and I could see he was overcome with disgust and shame. "Once I knew it was not some sort of bizarre dream, I threw her off of me. She laughed at me, her own father! Our daughter is mad, Olivia! Mad and dangerous! I threw her out of the house, and I do not know where she has gone. Perhaps to this captain she speaks of."

"He is dead, Isaiah. She shot him. In Roanoke. He has been dead for three years now."

"That's impossible, for I saw him earlier at my home. He stood outside the door waiting for her. She went to him when she left me. I locked the door behind her."

I took a sip of the dark claret. "Then you saw a ghost."

His eyes were even wider. "That's not all. She said—she cursed me, Olivia. Already I feel it taking effect. I am sick now, and I fear I shall die."

"You are being dramatic, Mr. Cottonwood. An angry woman—a madwoman—assaulted you. That is all. Do you really believe in curses? What woman has the power to do such things?"

"Don't talk to me about women, Mrs. Torrence."

"You expect me to help you after you confess to me that you have had carnal knowledge of our daughter? You expect me to assist you at all?" I smiled at him and watched the low light of the candelabra flicker. The candles burned low, and their red wax dripping made the moment that much more somber.

"You don't understand. I feel—my heart—the doctor says I am not supposed to have— Ahh...help me, Olivia."

I stood up as Isaiah slumped over the table, panting for breath and pounding at his chest. "I do understand you—and I curse you too! How dare you molest our daughter. How dare you refuse to help me! You thought you'd take advantage of my situation, but it has turned on you, hasn't it? Fate is a cruel mistress, Isaiah. This is why I did not want to marry you. You have always been unsteady. How does the saying go? 'A double-minded man is unstable in all his ways...'"

I rubbed his shoulder with my pale hand and whispered in his ear, "You are that man, and you are unstable in all your ways." All the emotions I had locked away, had carefully forbidden myself from feeling, rose to the surface. And despite my sudden tears, the emotion I felt most strongly was anger. All of it fell on Isaiah. My reasoning renounced its position as my chief counsel. Raw anger took control, and for the first time in my life, I welcomed it and allowed it to flow through me like dammed-up water through a pipe.

I sobbed, "I curse you, Isaiah—and your sons too. May you die, may they die in the prime of their life! May they feel happiness but have it stolen from them before they can fully possess it! I curse you for stealing my soul! You never cease to disappoint me, and now you would do this to me. You will not have what you seek. No peace for you or any of the Cottonwoods! Just as you did this to my blood, I curse your blood!

"I leave you now, Isaiah. I will never see you again. Except when they bury you. And they will bury you soon. Probably tomorrow."

Just then another guest joined us. It was Isla. "Mother, I can explain."

"What is there to say? I have cursed the man who hurt my daughter and stole my fortune. Now he is doubly cursed. See, he is dying. Leave him be, Isla. Why don't you go be with your captain in the Moonlight Garden before we have to leave this place?"

"You know about my sweet Captain?" Her voice sounded frail, quiet, pretty.

"The Moonlight Garden has always been a special place. Go now and leave your father to me."

***

I sputtered the sea water out of my lungs. How long had I been lying on this piece of foam, floating around the harbor? I'd woken up long enough to throw up, and now I was dying of thirst. Thankfully the storm had been during a warm season, or I was sure I would have died.

"Hey! Somebody! Help me!" I shouted about a hundred times. I heard nothing but the winds roaring and the waves crashing in response. Yelling into a storm was futile, so I waited for the waves to diminish and then tried again. The sun was rising now. How long had I been out here?

Long enough to know that Henri's prayer had been heard. God showed me what I needed to know, how the curse began and how I could break it. I had no doubt I would be found, because this had been his plan all along.

When the Coast Guard ship sailed in my direction, I cried. Not just because I had been found but because I knew how to break Olivia and Isla's curse. I would live to break it.

Carrie Jo! I love you! I know what to do now! I'm coming to you, baby!

Chapter Twelve—Carrie Jo

"I spent my whole life trying to prevent this dream walking, to prevent it from developing in you, but I failed—and I caused you great pain in the process," my mother said earnestly. "Please believe me when I tell you that I begged God a hundred times to take it from us. To take it from you. If you had seen the things my mother went through…she got so obsessed. All she wanted to do was sleep, and then one day she didn't wake up. I think the dreaming killed her, and I didn't want that for you. I thought if I followed the rules, you know, went to church, lived a holy life, if I became pure in the eyes of God, I could save you. I can't explain my reasoning. It all seems so crazy now."

"I can't believe this." The pain in my back worsened, but I didn't move. I stared at her. "You mean you knew what was happening to me and you didn't tell me? You knew all this time? I thought I was crazy. I thought you hated me!"

"I'm sorry, Carrie Jo. I am very sorry that I let you grow up not knowing what I knew, even if that wasn't very much."

A blast of wind moaned around the eave of the house. I heard the television bleeping a weather alert in the other room, but I was frozen to the spot. Rachel and Detra Ann were upstairs, laughing about something. The surreal moment lingered and I said, "How could you do that?"

She wrung her hands and covered her mouth. Finally she said, "All I can say is I am sorry."

"And I'm supposed to do what now?" I stood up. "Act like a 'sorry' makes it all better. That it erases it all? You're wrong, Momma. I'm not going to forget and..." I felt the need to get away, but I wasn't done giving her a piece of my mind. Kind Carrie Jo warned me to watch my mouth—that I would regret it if I said something stupid—but as sure as I was pregnant, I didn't listen to the voice of reason.

"I'm not asking you to do anything, Carrie Jo. Nothing at all. It's up to you if you want to accept my apology or not."

My hands were clenched into fists. My ponytail felt limp and my back pain kicked into high gear, but the tears were coming. There would be no stopping them now. "With Ginny, you knew I wasn't crazy? And that time when I kept seeing that old man in my dreams— the one who hurt himself? You knew those dreams were real and you let me sleep in that house anyway?"

"We had nowhere else to go! It was that or the street. Your dad left us high and dry. I had to take whatever we could get." Her eyes narrowed in frustration. "I'm not proud of what I did, the decisions I made. Not proud at all. I know it's too late to ask you to trust me now, but I could not let one more day go by without telling you that I am sorry. I am sorry about it all."

"What about my father? How come you never wanted to tell me about him? You know what that's like when you're a kid? What it's like now? He hates me, doesn't he?" The pain in my back grew more intense, and I could see flashes of light around the corners of my eyes. I put my hand on the table to steady myself.

"No! No, Carrie Jo. He doesn't hate you. He was afraid of us. Afraid of me. He's not a bad man, just a fearful one."

Angry words were poised at the tip of my tongue, but they didn't spring forth like I wanted them to. To my surprise, a splash of water landed on the floor between my legs. It felt warm and sticky. It didn't stop. My sandaled feet were all wet now. All I could think to say was, "Momma?"

She jumped out of the chair. "It's okay, Carrie Jo. This is normal. Your water broke. The baby is coming soon. We've got to get you back to the hospital." She put her arm around me and led me to the side door. "Oh, shoot! My car isn't here. Detra Ann? Rachel?" The girls bounded down the stairs, still smiling until they saw me.

"Does this mean what I think it means?" Detra Ann asked.

"Yes, her water broke. We've got to get her back to the hospital right now."

"Why did they send her home? I knew that was a mistake. Let's take my car." She ran to the living room, grabbed her purse and came back. "Let's do this, CJ. You've got this! Rachel? Would you mind cleaning this up?"

"Sure, I'll clean up and turn everything off. I'll meet y'all up there. Should I call Ashland and Henri?"

"Yep, that would be great." I hated the way everyone was talking so calmly. Like one of us had a baby every day. "See you there. Oh, and grab her suitcase by the front door!" Detra Ann said as she hurried me down the steps.

"Can't I change my clothes first? I look like I peed on myself."

"Um, no, girl. You don't have time for that. Once your water breaks, labor could start any—"

Just then I screamed. If I thought yesterday's contractions were anything to brag about, I was sorely mistaken. "Shoot! Shoot!" I said as I tried to remember how to breathe. I kicked myself again for not taking those Lamaze classes. "What do I do? What do I do, Momma?"

"Take slow, deep breaths when you can. I ain't gonna lie. It's gonna hurt like hell, but you'll survive."

"That's one hell of a pep talk, Deidre," Detra Ann scolded her.

"Well…. Oh, and don't push yet. For the love of God. It's not time to push. Let's get to the hospital first. We'll start timing the next one."

"Okay, okay," I said, breathing as slowly as I could. It was hard as heck to do with my heart pounding and my pulse racing. Detra Ann practically shoved me in the backseat and began backing the car down the driveway like a wild woman. *Should I tell her my purse is hanging out the door? Breathe, breathe, breathe!*

"Too bad it's not a girl. We could call her Jasmine, in honor of the storm," Detra Ann said, smiling at me in the rearview mirror.

"Never," I promised her. "But Ashland would love that. I hope Rachel got a hold of him."

"Don't you worry about it, CJ. He'll be there." Detra Ann shouted at me as she ran a red light.

Deidre gasped and grabbed my hand. "Sweet Lord!"

"Get your watch ready. I feel another one coming. I'm sorry about your backseat, Detra Ann."

"Son of a b! Did you see that guy? I don't care about the backseat, but don't have the baby in my car! Jasmine deserves better."

Between pants and twists of pain I panted, "I'm—not-calling-her—Jasmine. Oh God, oh God!"

Detra Ann hit a curb trying to avoid a car. It was like being on a painful bumper car ride. My mother prayed beside me the whole time. Detra Ann grinned like a maniac when she wasn't honking at someone or threatening to cut their body parts off.

"Here we are! Pulling in the driveway now!" she yelled, forgetting once again that I was pregnant and not hard of hearing.

"Great! Perfect timing! Here comes another one!"

"Three minutes apart! That baby will be here soon!" My mother opened her door, rescued my purse and practically dragged me out of the backseat. "Hey! My daughter is having a baby! Like right now!"

"Momma! That's an ambulance guy. Not a nurse!"

It didn't matter. She was going to make sure someone helped me, and all I could do was hold my breath and hope the pain quit. A dark-haired young man squatted down in front of me. "What's your name?"

"Carrie Jo. It's Carrie Jo."

"Okay, Carrie Jo. I've got a chair here. Think you can stand so we can get you in it?"

"In just a second." I held my breath and waited for the contraction to let up.

"Don't hold your breath. Try to breathe through them. It will help with the pain. That's better. Take your time. I'll wait." Over his shoulder he told the approaching nurse what was happening.

"I think I can stand up now."

"They are three minutes apart," Deidre told the nurse as she pushed me through the hospital doors. "And her water broke."

"Sounds like we have a baby on the way. If it's a girl you could name her Jasmine."

I rolled my eyes at Detra Ann, who ran along beside me. "Never," I mouthed to her.

My clothes were drenched, my forehead was covered in sweat, and I was exhausted already. "Detra Ann, call Ashland, please. I need him here."

"I will. Deidre you stay with her while I find out what's going on."

Before I knew it, the nurse had me in the elevator and we were headed to the fifth floor. No long registration process for me. "Got no time to waste. The doctor says to bring you up now. Baby's coming! It's going to be okay. We're going to get you an IV started, he'll check to see how far you've dilated and then we'll go from there. How does that sound?"

"Like a dream. I'd like to wait for my husband."

The nurse, a young woman with pretty, soft-looking brown hair, smiled sympathetically. "Hopefully he will make it in time. But either way, I think you will meet your baby soon." Sure enough, another nurse came in quickly and had me rigged up to the IV in no time.

Dr. Gary arrived, apologizing that he had sent me home. A quick examination confirmed it. "Eight centimeters dilated. It's almost time."

"I know!" I practically screamed at him as another contraction, the strongest so far, took my breath away.

"How about an epidural to help with the pain?"

"Please? I would love one." All my pledges to "go natural" went out the window. I wondered if breast-feeding would hit the chopping block too.

"Be right back," Dr. Gary said as he pulled the blanket back down.

"Momma, please find out where Ashland is—he needs to get here."

Detra Ann walked back in, her phone in her hand. I could tell by the look on her face that something was wrong.

Something was dead wrong.

"Ashland is missing. Henri saw him fall in the water. He's with the authorities. They are looking for him now." She flew to my side and rubbed my hand. "You listen to me, Carrie Jo Stuart. We are not going to entertain anything negative about Ashland, you hear me? He is going to be fine. Right now, you have his baby to think about! I know you want to cry and fall apart, but you can't! You don't have that luxury! Let's have this baby so we can find out what's happening."

"Detra Ann, no! I can't—you have to go be with Henri! Help him find Ash! Please!"

Dr. Gary heard the shouting and came in; a nurse was tying on his face mask. "What is this? What's going on in here? Trying to have a baby, people."

"You don't understand, Dr. Gary. Carrie Jo's husband, Ashland, has disappeared off his boat. He's in the water and they haven't found him. But they will!"

"You had to tell her that now?" He sat on the rolling chair and rolled to my side. "I know you wish you could be doing something else right now, but this child needs you. Your son needs you. Let's welcome him into the world and make sure he's healthy. That's the number one thing right now, got it?"

Still in shock from the news about Ashland, I said, "Yes, that's the number one thing. Ashland's baby. Oh God, please protect him. Momma!"

"Yes, darling."

"I know you wanted to be in here, but I need you praying for Ashland. Let Detra Ann stay with me, and you go pray. When Rachel gets here, get her praying too. Please, Momma. Pray your very hardest!" I cried as the sweat poured off my forehead.

"What's the air on?" Detra Ann asked the nurse. Without waiting she checked the room thermostat and immediately dropped it. It didn't do any good because just then the lights went out. In the momentary silence I could hear the winds rattling the windows of the hospital like moaning ghosts demanding to be let in.

"I've had enough of ghosts! You hear me? Enough!"

Dr. Gary stared at me. "Carrie Jo, are you with me? Nurse, check her IV bag. I did not order anything that would make her hallucinate."

Detra Ann assured him I was fine, that I was just worried about Ashland, and then the labor began in earnest. "Okay, let's check. Yes, fully dilated. That was fast once you got started. That's a good thing. Some people have the worst time opening up. Let's see…oh yes, I see a little head already. Now it's important that you push when I tell you to push, okay. Are you in pain?"

"No pain, just a lot of pressure. Can I push yet?"

"Let me get in position. Okay, let's push."

I sat up and held my knees, pushing with all my might. *This isn't right. This shouldn't be happening. Not without my husband. Ashland, I love you. Where are you!*

I need you right now!

Chapter Thirteen—Carrie Jo

"Of course you know this will open you up to a ton of lawsuits now, right?" Libby said, frowning at Ashland. "And that you've just signed away seventy-five percent of your net worth? That's a big deal, Ashland. I'm not sure you understand how far this decision reaches. This could haunt you for the rest of your life."

Libby couldn't know how apropos her choice of words was. "We hope so," he answered cryptically.

"I just can't believe this. You're normally so level-headed. Is this because of your son? Or something else?" She glanced at me as if I were the culprit. I kept my face completely expressionless.

"Yes and no," he said. "That's all I can tell you. I appreciate your help with all this."

"I still don't get it. I don't get this whole thing. I need a vacation." She tapped her head with her pen in frustration. "It might be the last one any of us take."

"Don't tell us you're breaking up with us, Libby," I said with a smirk. Ashland laughed, and boy, did that sound good. Money was all Libby really cared about. Well, money and stealing my husband. Now she would lose on both counts.

"Two of these claimants can't even prove they are related to your family. You do know that, right?" He nodded, and I could tell he was starting to feel a bit aggravated about this whole conversation. "This sets a bad standard, Ashland. Not just for you but for many of the older families here in Mobile. You haven't heard the last of this, I'm afraid. Not by a long shot."

"This is the right thing to do, Libby," he replied. "Not just for us but for everyone involved. I know you don't understand my decision, our decision, but this is it. This is how it should have always been."

Libby shook her head, her stylish bob swinging as she did. With perfectly manicured hands she stamped the documents and folded them up neatly. She placed them in the thick manila envelopes and looked at us like we were both out of our heads.

"As long as you know what you're doing. Who am I to say?"

Ashland and I walked out of the building and stepped into the warm sunshine. It was hard to believe that a major storm had blown through here just two weeks ago. Most of the fallen oaks had been removed, but there were plenty of houses missing shingles, windows—you name it. I closed my eyes for a moment as we stood outside the car. I felt lighter, like an unseen weight had been lifted off my shoulders, and I was sure Ashland felt the same way. After a minute, I poked him in the side. "One more stop before the event, babe. Can't daydream now."

"I'll leave all the dreaming to you."

"As well you should. Speaking of which, Deidre says she'll meet us at Seven Sisters with Baby Boy. Did Mr. Chapman from the city call you? He said the sign arrived and they'll be installing it in front of the house today. I can't believe Seven Sisters won't be called

Seven Sisters anymore, but I like the sound of the Beaumont-Cottonwood Manor. It sounds…right. Oh, I almost forgot. Doreen and Rachel are coming too. I can't believe this is going down without Henri and Detra Ann. Are you sure we can't wait?"

"We'll throw them a huge party when they get back. And yes, I'm sure this can't wait. You know, I've heard people talk about getting married in Vegas, but I've never actually met someone who did. Can't believe they went without us," he said with a smile.

I laughed. "I can. Those two don't need us there. They'll have Elvis and Marilyn Monroe as their witnesses. I promise you this, though, Detra Ann's mother is going to have a nervous breakdown when she finds out they got hitched. She's the only girl in that family, and I'm sure Cynthia's always dreamed of throwing her a big wedding."

"Probably so."

He turned the car down the forgotten road. His Jeep found every bump and pothole, but it didn't matter. We were on a mission. It was hard to believe fall was here, with the way the sun beamed down on us. The balmy weather made me want to slip off my shoes and prop my feet up on the dash, but now wasn't the time for that. The Jeep came to a stop, and in the distance I could hear the river lapping against the sandy riverbank.

"This is about it," I said. "I remember seeing this place in a dream. There was once an old oak tree that stood there. Isla used to climb it and watch the boys swim. The Delta Queen used to roll along here, and just a way down was where she embarked the night Calpurnia landed in the water."

"When we ceded the house to the city, I thought that would be the end of all this. I hope this truly is the end. Do you think it will be?" he asked me, grabbing the roses out of the backseat.

I slid my sunglasses up to the top of my head. "No matter what happens, this is the right thing to do. I am proud of you, babe, for wanting to make it right. I think the ghosts of the past will know that you've tried, that we've tried, and they'll accept that."

He squeezed my hand, and we walked down the steep hillside to the riverbank. "I don't know how we managed to talk the city into changing the name of the house. Usually this kind of thing takes years. The Beaumont-Cottonwood Plantation. That has a nice ring to it, doesn't it?"

"Yep, it does." He handed me some roses. Thankfully, the florist had been nice enough to clip the thorns from the stems. I took the flowers, and we stood by the water with our heads bowed. "You ready?" I asked him quietly.

"Yes, I am. Finally." With his eyes closed, he tilted his head up toward the blue sky.

"Dear Lord, my wife and I ask you to lift the curse that was placed upon my family all those years ago. I know that wrongs were done, many wrongs. I know that many people were hurt as a result of those wrongs. Although I did not personally do these things, I take responsibility for them as the current representative of our family. I repent, Lord. We stole from others, we made our brothers slaves, we hid our secrets and refused to repent of them. Many of us did murder and many other sinful things in your sight. But I, Ashland James Stuart, do repent, Lord, on behalf of my sinful ancestors. I am sorry." I squeezed his hand as a tear rolled down his cheek.

As he wiped his face with his hands, his eyes looked even bluer through the tears. Still speaking to God, he said, "I have given the moment to the people who deserved it. I have a clean conscience, God. I have given the house the name it deserves. I hope this is enough. But if it's not, please tell me what to do and I will do it. If not for me, Lord, for my son and my wife. She is innocent."

"No, I am not so innocent either," I said to Ashland. Then I spoke to God as Ash had, toward the blue sky. "I have been bitter and unforgiving toward the people I love. I had no idea that you were trying to help me, that my mother was doing what she thought she should. I was wrong to hate her. For that I am sorry. I do not know how I am related to Muncie yet, if at all. But if I am, I will not be ashamed to call him my cousin. Or uncle. Or whatever he may be. I accept him. Thank you for keeping Ashland safe. Thank you for our family."

It was my turn to cry now. I put my face in Ashland's chest and cried my heart out. When my tears had flowed, I prepared to throw the flowers in the water as a kind of tribute to the many Cottonwoods, Beaumonts and others caught up in the centuries-long curse, but I froze. Standing on the water, just as she would have described Reginald Ball as walking out like "Holy Jesu," was Calpurnia. She was not the sickly, defeated girl I remembered from my dreams but happy and smiling. She walked toward us, the hem of her coral gown skimming the water.

"Ashland, do you see her?"

"Yes," he whispered without looking at me. She floated closer, and the bright sunlight sparkled in her intricate hairstyle. With shaking fingers, Ashland handed her a red rose. Her fingers never touched his, but she accepted the flower from him. "Be at peace," she whispered to him. She smiled at me too, and the coral earrings bobbed at her ears. Suddenly, Muncie stood beside her. He was no longer Muncie the boy but Janjak the man, the teacher in a three-piece suit. He took her hand, and I held out a flower to him with shaking fingers.

"Be at peace," he said to me in a soothing, rich voice. Together they stepped back on the water and soon faded away with smiles on their faces. We breathed a sigh of relief, but then there were others, walking to us across the river.

Isla came next. She wore her powder blue gown with the full lacy sleeves. I could feel Ashland tense beside me, but he offered her the rose. "Forgive me, cousin," he said in a sincere voice.

"Be at peace," she said. She accepted the rose and vanished immediately. Others came too, Christine, Delilah and finally Olivia.

I had seen Olivia only once in a dream, but I knew Ashland had seen much of her, either in dreams or as a ghost. He handed her a rose as she drew close, her hair still upswept with not a hair out of place. She looked at the flower for a moment and leaned closer to his face. "So you are the curse-breaker? Be at peace, cousin." She too vanished as Isla had done.

We tossed the rest of the roses on the water and watched them float away down the Mobile River.

"The curse is broken, Ashland. It is over, at last!"

"Yes, I believe it is. Thank God!"

"I was so nervous. I hardly expected to see Janjak or anyone!"

"Me too!" We were all smiles.

"We better get going. Little AJ will be missing you," I said with a smile.

"I can't believe you named our son Ashland James."

"Well, if it was good enough for you, it's good enough for him. At least it's not Jasmine."

"What do you have against Jasmine?"

"Nothing, really. Maybe we'll consider it for our daughter."

"Daughter? Whoa! We just gave away all our money. Maybe we should slow down on growing the family for a while."

"No way. We've got to restock the family tree, babe." I put my arms around his neck and kissed him.

"And what good stock it is too," he purred playfully. As I kissed him I pretended I didn't hear a giggle or two coming from the direction of that old oak tree.

"You hear anything?" I asked cautiously.

"Nope. Let's go."

We drove out of the woods and down the bumpy, beaten path, back to the road that would lead us to the future. Our good future. It *was* going to be a good one. A curse-free one.

I felt overwhelmed with gratitude. "Thank you," I whispered to no one in particular. I knew everyone who was supposed to hear it would.

Author's Note

It's the last page of the book and you want to close it, but you just can't. The characters are not merely names on a page. You know them, understand them—you'll miss them. You were with them throughout the journey, a witness to their heartaches and triumphs. You walked through the Moonlight Garden, swam in the Mobile River and explored the old house. You have unanswered questions. There should be more to this story!

I hope you feel this way about the *Seven Sisters* books. If you do, that is the best thing I could ever hope for. I know I do. Like you, it is difficult for me to say goodbye to these friends, but at least they will live on for us in the pages of these books and we can visit them again and again. For me, if you miss them, that's proof that I've done my job. I told the story I wanted to tell, and I hope you enjoyed it.

I remember when I began to write Chapter One of the first book. I had such a compulsion to put it all on paper. It was during a difficult time in my personal life, but at the end of every day I found an escape—a forgotten plantation called Seven Sisters. And there…Calpurnia waited to be found. Muncie hoped to be loved. Carrie Jo wanted to be understood. It was a delight to make that happen for the characters, and by doing that I made it through a major transition in my life. I highly recommend writing as therapy.

Although I was born in Antigua in the British West Indies, generations of my family have called Mobile home, and that's where I spent much of my time as a child. I used to love visiting my grandmother; she lived in a rural part of the county. She had the most amazing old house in the country, complete with wisteria vines, bushy hydrangeas and, of course, forgotten paths in the woods that led to mysterious places. We always came back to Mobile, no matter where my military family traveled, and I loved every one of those returns. I've had the privilege of visiting dozens of states and have even traveled overseas but this…this mosquito-laden bowl of humidity has always been home. And it will continue to be so.

I enjoyed weaving real places and people into my stories. It was a delight to share downtown Mobile with you, and if you ever get the chance, come visit. I joke about the skeeters and the heat, but that's nothing compared to the people, the food and the architecture.

One of the biggest questions I am asked is this: "Is Seven Sisters a real place?" Answering that is difficult. It's a yes and a no. As far as I know, there was never a plantation in Mobile called Seven Sisters, but we've lost so many of those old houses, so who knows? I did base much of the structure of the house on real houses: the Oakleigh Manor in Mobile and the Bragg-Mitchell Mansion. You can tour both of those!

As far as dream catchers go, maybe people can go back in time and dream about the past. I have enough room in my belief system to allow for a bit of magic. Don't you? I'll let you make up your own mind about ghosts and such.

So what lies ahead? I have a few things in the works. As I mentioned on my Facebook page a few months ago, I am working on the screenplay for Seven Sisters. I think Carrie Jo deserves a movie, don't you?

I have also completed a historical fiction series about Queen Nefertiti. It's called the Desert Queen series and I'm very happy with it. If you fancy a bit of adventure in ancient Egypt, check it out.

At the moment, I am swimming my way through an urban fantasy called Sirens Gate. It's about an angsty siren, her human boyfriend and a host of other supernatural creatures who descend on Mobile's Dauphin Island. It's so fun to write about mermaids and vampires!

I also have a new spooky plantation series coming this fall, called the Sugar Hill series. There will be three books in that one: The Wife of the Left Hand, The Ramparts, and Blood by Candlelight. I can't wait to introduce you to the Dufresne family and take you through their plantation, Sugar Hill. Like Seven Sisters, the series will be chock full of Southern folklore and historical places.

Thanks again for staying with me through this series. I appreciate all your kind words, the reviews and the emails.

Don't forget to sign up for my mailing list or follow me on Amazon or BookBub so you can get the newest release information right in your inbox.

See y'all soon.

M.L. Bullock

Read more from M.L. Bullock

The Seven Sisters Series

Seven Sisters
Moonlight Falls on Seven Sisters
Shadows Stir at Seven Sisters
The Stars that Fell
The Stars We Walked Upon
The Sun Rises Over Seven Sisters

The Desert Queen Series

The Tale of Nefret
The Falcon Rises
The Kingdom of Nefertiti
The Song of the Bee-Eater (forthcoming)

The Sugar Hill Series (forthcoming)

Wife of the Left Hand
The Ramparts
Blood By Candlelight

The Sirens Gate Series (forthcoming)

The Mermaid's Gift
The Blood Feud
The Wrath of Minerva
The Lorelei Curse
The Fortunate Star

The Southern Gothic Series

Being with Beau

To receive updates on her latest releases,
visit her website at MLBullock.com
and subscribe to her mailing list.

Made in the USA
San Bernardino, CA
14 October 2016